Herbert Dickinson Ward

The Burglar Who Moved Paradise

Herbert Dickinson Ward

The Burglar Who Moved Paradise

ISBN/EAN: 9783744790826

Printed in Europe, USA, Canada, Australia, Japan

Cover: Foto ©Andreas Hilbeck / pixelio.de

More available books at **www.hansebooks.com**

Hold on tight, Miss (page 22)

THE BURGLAR

WHO MOVED PARADISE

BY HERBERT D. WARD

BOSTON AND NEW YORK
HOUGHTON, MIFFLIN AND COMPANY
The Riverside Press, Cambridge
1897

The Riverside Press, Cambridge, Mass., U. S. A.
Electrotyped and Printed by H. O. Houghton & Co.

DRAMATIS PERSONÆ OF THE OLD MAID'S PARADISE

SCENE — *Fairharbor, a town on the Massachusetts Coast.*

Hero . . . . . A Cottage.
Heroine . . . . Corona (*Owner of the Cottage*).
Maid to Corona . . . Puelvir.
Brother to Corona . . Tom.
Sister-in-Law to Corona . Susy.
Niece to Corona . . A Baby.
Friends to Corona . { Mary.
{ Effie.
A Builder . . . Mr. Timbers.
Boy to Corona . . . Zero.
A Dog . . . . Matthew Launcelot.
A Horse . . . . Lady of Shalott.
Neighbors.
Sub-Hero . . . A Widower.

NOTE

It may be remembered by a few of my friendly readers that I had, some years ago, the pleasure of recording for them the experiences of an old maid who built a matched board cottage at the seaside, and with various episodes more or less interesting to her friends, but all of them absorbing to her, lived in it happily ever after. The adventures of Corona, of Puelvir her maid, of the Raspberry Man, who wooed Puelvir unsuccessfully, and married a widow with four; of a boy, a dog, a horse, and a burglar, all of them closely intertwined with Corona's history, were conscientiously related, and have been amiably considered by a too generous public.

As the volumes to which I allude are no longer recent publications it may be prudent to recall more minutely that Corona had been robbed of a five-hundred-dollar bond, and that in the early autumn following this incident, while she sat calculating the costs of her non-recovery (it amounted, I remember, to four hundred and eighty-two dollars and thirty-six and a half cents) a gentleman had arrived unexpectedly at the Old Maid's Paradise. He was a widower and an old acquaintance, and he helped Corona do the sum about the detectives. It was September, and the glory of that which is irrevocably passing away was on the sea and on the harbor shore. Corona and the widower sat together and talked of friendship and the present very prettily. Corona declined to discuss either the past or the future.

Her biographer, indeed, raised the question, "Had the most dangerous burglar of all climbed up to Paradise?" But the query was never answered. It has often been my wish, and at times my intention, to reply to this question myself by further annals of the history of Paradise. Having been unable to carry out this design I am happy to give way to another plan and pen. To the following sympathetic effort to represent the burglar in Paradise, I offer my heartiest good will, asking of my readers of an earlier time only that they extend to this little story the same kindness of heart which once they offered to mine.

ELIZABETH STUART PHELPS.

AUTHOR'S PREFACE

THE following narrative, it is needless to say, is entirely from the man's point of view. It may be the fact that the woman sees only the heraldic colors, and the man the marshaling of arms upon the shield. However that may be, it is well to have the family coat-of-arms presented from every point of view. Again, from a feminine standpoint, it is to be expected that the "Sub-hero" should be of the masculine denomination. But a man is not to be eternally snubbed, even if he is only a lay figure in a story. And so, by the privilege of being the last writer on the subject, I have seen to it that the despised "sub" has arisen past all intermediate stages until he plays the principal part to the heroine in this little drama of life.

A house makes a very good hero for an

"old maid" to beguile an audience with. But we are sure that if we promote the man and degrade the dwelling to its proper place in the *dramatis personæ*, and drop the "old maid" altogether, the play will have truer proportions and move from scene to scene with more heroic satisfaction.

HERBERT D. WARD.

CONTENTS

THE BURGLAR WHO MOVED PARADISE

CHAPTER I

THE WIDOWER

ALTHOUGH there has been no evidence of the fact up to the time of this writing, nevertheless the widower had a name. Why there should have been any mystery about it is hard to explain. Perhaps an exaggerated feminine delicacy forbade its being published. Perhaps that spirit of aggravation, which might be called the stimulator of curiosity and which belongs peculiarly to the gentler sex, prompted its suppression.

For the widower's name was neither uncomfortably suggestive, like Washington Sudds, Esq., or Mr. Wiley T. Rickey, nor was it aristocratic like Reginald Guelph de Somerset. On the other hand it was not

elemental like Smith nor rare like Toxteth.
Suffice it to say that the widower was a man
of the better classes of intelligence and means.
His name (why juggle with the subject any
longer?) was Alexander Hensleigh.   The
pedigree of Alexander is not difficult to
trace; but his patronymic had descended
to him through English, and after these
through Nova Scotian ancestors until, like
all of the best things, the name and the race
had become bone of our Republic.

It was March, and all that the third month
of the year implies to the city of Boston.
There had been a storm at sea and a blizzard
on land.   Vessels had been driven on shore;
cars had been blockaded in the streets.   It
was the third day of the storm, and the old
Eastern Depot congealed under a draught,
the quality of which could not have been
produced without the boundaries of New
England.

The 10.45 Fairharbor train was waiting
on the track.   The engine was just backing
to make the connection, and it was within

two or three minutes of the starting time. A tall gentleman with fur cap and ulster, black beard inclining to gray, and eager eyes, paced the platform nervously. He had just run through the whole train for the third time, staring each of the lady passengers almost out of countenance. He was now engaged in consulting the station clock, and now in glaring at the gateway. When he did not bite his mustache he made no pretense of disguising his disappointment. He scowled at every one who was unfortunate enough to cross his line of vision.

There was hardly a minute left. The conductor with the white mustache, whom all the Fairharbor people knew with a more or less degree of train intimacy, stood ready, watch in hand. The engine wheezed impatiently.

"All aboard!" shouted the conductor.

At that moment a tall figure walked through the gate. It did not hurry. It glided composedly along until it reached the rear car of the train. The conductor

tipped his hat and smiled a welcome, for
he recognized a favorite summer passenger.
He helped the lady up, and then lifted his
hand. The engineer opened the throttle
slowly.

There was one vacant seat and Corona
dropped into it. Corona. was a striking-
looking woman. She was a strong, mobile
blonde, with chestnut hair, and a firm
mouth that looked a little severe in repose, -
and that curved and fascinated when in
action. Her eyes could be as cold as a
tempered blade or as affectionate as a violet,
according to her mood. Corona was tall
and trig. She was highly bred in every
movement, perhaps too reserved to suit a
chance acquaintance. But the old friend
might once in a while catch a gleam of
forget-me-not in her eyes, a flush of fidelity
in her cheeks, a rose of passion in her lips,
a constancy that illumined her whole countenance, which proclaimed, in spite of her
New England bearing, the woman for whose
attainment a man might well spend his life.

New England women have been much misunderstood and carelessly called self-sufficient. But their manner is only a matter of indirect radiation. It is healthier because it is so. What manner of householder is he who wants the furnace continually on draught, blistering the pure atmosphere of the home, or of the hearth? Corona had enough warmth in her for those she loved, and for the one elect who should discover her to herself and to him, even though she did look a little unapproachable in her present attitude.

During the winter Corona lived in one of the Boston suburbs with Tom, her brother, and Susy, her sister-in-law. Tom and Susy had a baby, and something was always the matter with the baby. This time it was deferentially called bad dreams. No one had slept the night before, and Corona had to take the early train with Tom in order to be driven to their little station. This morning Tom was late, and Corona had almost missed her Fairharbor train. As she looked out of the window, she gave the impression of being absorbed by eternal verities.   One would have thought that she was analyzing the last novel by Tolstoi, with its unquestionable moral aim, and its questionable immoral characters, or that she was wondering whether the time had come for the organization of a society for the propagation of Buddhism on Beacon Street.   But Corona had a sane mind.   It was occupied with nothing less than the circumstance that her summer house was leaking.

Zero had leisurely written her about it the week after he had found it out.   Zero was Corona's boy-of-all-laziness, one of the most important members of her summer Paradise, the currier of her horse and favors, an institution for the absorption of extra doughnuts and uneaten desserts, a part of her sea life, and as necessary as the stove in the kitchen or the rocks upon the beach.   And Zero kept the keys of Paradise in winter.

Corona proceeded now to draw forth from her muff this boy's letter, and to meditate

further upon the humid problems which
dampen every owner and builder of his own
house at some time or other in his ardent
career. Corona had put off her regular
midwinter trip to Fairharbor on account of
the baby. But a leak was different. Baby
or no baby, a leak must be mended, or
patched, or darned. This was Corona's first
own leak, and she was vigorously wondering
what ought to be done under the circumstances. So she had telegraphed Mr. Timbers to meet her at Paradise at half past
twelve. Mr. Timbers was the builder of
the Old Maid's Paradise. And she had
telegraphed Zero to harness up The Lady
and meet her when the train came in. The
Lady of Shalott was Corona's horse. Un-
like her mistress, the horse was not a summer guest. She stayed among the winter
people in Zero's care. But all Corona's
calculations stopped with telegrams. She
looked from the letter to the white snow
outside, helplessly awaiting a practical inspiration. She wished — she wished —

"Is this seat engaged? May I? — may I, Corona?"

She started at the familiar voice, and glanced around and up. A tall man devoured the face now flushed out of its serenity, and looked down. It was a year ago last fall since he had bade her good-by on the porch of her own house by the September sea. Not for a moment since had the picture which her last attitude had etched upon his heart faded from his imagination.

"May I?" he repeated gently. She saw that his lips quivered, and a great wave of pity for him obscured in spite of herself her startled eyes. She moved closer to the window and automatically held out her hand.

"Where — where do you come from? You *man*, you?"

Alexander Hensleigh took his seat and took her hand, and laughed softly with the content of a successful hunter. The dream of eighteen months — the dream to be near her, to touch her hand, to watch her face, to hear her voice, to be warmed by her smile

— had now come to pass. Only he who
has loved in doubt and distance can understand the bitterness, the happiness, the un-
certainty, the hope, of such long waiting.
A hundred times a day he knew that he
would never see her again, and that either
he or she would die, and that such bliss as
only she might bestow could never be for
him. And as many times he knew that he
should see her, and he felt that the one
desire of his heart must be the logical earnest of its fulfillment.

Thus two people meet in a crowd. To
the passenger across the aisle, if he notices
them at all, the two are like cinders that
have accidentally touched in a draught.
But only they know that an epoch, as important to them as the creation, has over-
taken their lives. Corona looked at her old
friend with a mixture of resentment and
admiration for the masterfulness by which
she had been entrapped.

"I wrote you," he said quietly, "about
three weeks ago, to expect me."

"I did n't get it."

"Your brother told me this morning that he had a letter for you somewhere. I remember he smiled in a peculiar way."

"I 'll never trust Tom as long as I live again with my mail!"

"I hope you never will have to," Hensleigh insinuated gently. "I have brought it myself." He took the letter out of his overcoat pocket, showed her the address, and then put it back.

"So Tom told you that I was to be on this train?" Corona tapped her finger on the back of her hand. "I see it all. It 's a conspiracy. I hope you feel satisfied with this underhand performance!" she flashed in her old way. "Besides, I 'll take my letter."

"I certainly do. No, you won't." This was spoken with a quiet assurance that startled Corona more than anything else could have done. She glanced up at his face hurriedly. She read there the calm expression of one who was master of the situation. She felt like crying out aloud in

protest. But those lips that had now become firm, those insistent eyes, told her that
the time had come at last when she could
no more escape him than a bird can escape
from a locked cage. And she respected
him, womanlike, all the more for it.

Alexander Hensleigh settled back in his
seat comfortably. For a man who had
finally severed every strand that bound him
to his past life, and to whom this moment
was as important as the sun after a week's
tempest is to the driven ship, he certainly
exhibited few signs of anxiety. Many
months of self-distrust had been succeeded
by a kind of exaltation as the woman beside
him stepped upon the train.

He took Zero's letter from her fingers
exactly as if he owned her, and as if he
were not guilty of unpardonable imperti-
nence. This she helplessly allowed.

"It is from Zero. You can read it," she
said. She caught her breath, wondering
what was coming next. Of what audacity
was this widower not capable in his present

mood? He opened the letter, and read as
follows. The letter was written on a spiled
half of a store sheet of paper ruled blue:—

MISS KORONOH: i want to tell you that
yure Hous is leekin badly in the Pallor.
You kin almost Katch cunners There. i
Think you ort to Sea about it. No one hez
broke in yet.

Your Obedyuntly,   ZERO.

They both laughed, and their eyes met
merrily.

"It is so good to laugh," he said, "and
I thank God that neither Matthew Launcelot nor Puelvir is here to matronize you this
time. I want you all to myself for once in
my life."

"You'll find Zero at the other end," she
suggested demurely. "I've built a kitchen
since you were at Paradise," she added,
with the charming irrelevance of a woman
who will go to any length to change the
subject.

"Ah!" replied Hensleigh without enthusiasm.

"Yes, a brand-new kitchen, with a room on top for Puelvir. She calls it her house; she moved in those maroon and indigo curtains of hers before the carpenters were out — it's perfectly delightful. The old kitchen is the dining-room now, and there's a lovely storeroom. You can't think how happy she is!"

"Really? I'm glad *Puelvir* is happy," answered Hensleigh with dark significance. "Here's Zero's letter," he continued in an anxious and aimless tone.

Their hands touched as he gave her the letter back. She did not immediately withdraw her fingers as they were hidden under her muff. Strange how lonely and helpless she felt when she stepped aboard that train! Life was as bleak as the sky to her then. Now summer seemed suddenly to have sprung into existence. Indeed, at that moment the sun blazed out for the first time after these many terrible days of storm.

As usual, on the Fairharbor branch, the car was full. The conductor with the white mustache took up their tickets, and after a pleasant word passed on. The marshes of Lynn, hidden by snow and ice, began to glitter in the new sun. Even the bay beyond assumed an air of cheerfulness entirely inconsistent with the tempestuous month. Hensleigh leaned over to pull the shade down, in order to shut out the reflection of the light, the more glaring because the more unexpected. But Corona shook her head and looked out dreamily.

Then the man bent close to her, and their faces were both lighted by the sun. He whispered, and the rumble of the train drowned the sound of his voice to every other ear but hers: —

"You know, Corona, why I have come?"

"Why? How should I? Why?" She made a desperate effort to look unconscious, but her risen color belied her affectation. This sign of weakness made her angry with herself, and then with him.

"I have loved you too long, Corona, for you not to know it."

"I suppose that is the reason you left me sixteen years ago."

"Now, now, Corona, don't let us quarrel! Time is too precious. We are too old."

"Speak for yourself, sir!" frigidly.

"I did n't mean that. You know I did n't — I meant" —

"I 'm afraid it 's no use, Mr. Hensleigh; we always did quarrel, and we always shall. Do you think you can neglect a woman for the best part of her life — marry somebody else — and then come back, swear eternal love, and expect her to fall into your arms like a pet poodle? The East and the West are different, sir." She brought the shade down sharply to hide her emotion.

By this time all the confidence of the few moments ago had died out of the man's heart. He bent his head and bit his lips to control his words. As he was silent longer than she expected — for one side of a quar-

rel is n't much fun, even at the rate of thirty
miles an hour — Corona glanced at him
with that intuitive sideways motion that
makes even the most commonplace of women
mysterious to masculine minds. She saw
her old friend's dejection, and she pitied
him for the second time.

"I have given up everything, Corona,"
he began again gravely. "I have sold my
house, disposed of my business, and have
come East to stay — to stay, Corona, forever with you — if you will have me, dear."

It was now her turn to be silent. This
was a devotion that she could not taunt.

"Let me think," she said, with a swift
glance of confidence that made a man of
him again. "Ask me later — Ah, there's
the sea. How beautiful! How happy!"

. . . .

"Here you are, Miss Corona. Take you
right over!" The pilot of the Fairharbor
stage jumped forward as Corona stepped
out. The air was salt and cold, but how
fresh and pure! Nobody noticed her com-

panion, but Corona, as he helped her off
the car, had leaned upon his arm more
heavily than one would expect a hearty,
modern woman to do. She had also given
him a look of gratitude, so swift that not
even the stage-driver had noticed it. The
snow was heaped high around the station.

"Take you over safe as a dory on a float!
Got new runners on this morning. This is
the worst we ever had. Snow draws three
feet everywhere on a level," insisted the
driver affably.

"My own carriage is here to meet me."
Corona spoke with the dignity that only a
horse-holder can assume. " Zero is here to
meet me."

"He! he!! he!!!" irreverently snickered
the driver.

"Isn't Zero here as I telegraphed?"
Corona asked hastily.

"He's there, all right, on the other side,
but—he! he!! he!!!"

Corona motioned to her companion as she
hurried over. It was true, there was her

faithful Zero — a boy of about fifteen — standing up to his hips in snow at the head of a prancing, snorting, kicking horse. Apparently The Lady of Shalott was doing the best she could to stand on her head. In the pursuance of this noble effort she had floundered into a six-foot drift and was rapidly drawing the boy out of sight.   And behind that horse was a *buggy*.

"Why, Zero!" exclaimed the proprietor of the outfit.

"Hay?" spluttered Zero blankly.

"Oh, I forgot," said Corona, "the boy is as deaf as a boulder, and I forget it every spring."

"I'm dum glad ye 've come, miss," said the hapless boy, bobbing the snow out of his eyes.   "I thought ye had n't come and wuz wonderin' how to get in.   I've hed one policeman and three men holdin' of this hoss, and bin two hours gettin' here.   It wuz orfurl!   Whoa, there!   Whoa!"

"But, Zero, why did n't you put her into a sleigh?"

"Hay?"

"Sleigh! Sleigh!"

"Way?" asked Zero intelligently. "Yes, I hed to walk her all the way."

The engine at this crisis let off steam, and the boy lost his footing as The Lady dashed deeper into the drift. One degree of angle more and the buggy would have been capsized.

"No, *sleigh?*"

"You did n't say nothin' about sleigh. You said to bring down yer team, and here she is, the hull of it, and I got all I want of it, you kin betchyer life on that." The tears began to come to the desperate boy's eyes.

"Zero, I am surprised" —

"Wise?" said Zero. "I ain't so wise as you be. Me an' The Lady are both blarsted fools to be here anyhow."

"Dear me!" said Corona, "the boy is growing up. He is learning to swear." When she had left, last fall, Zero was as mild as a clam.

By this time the buggy would have collapsed had not the widower plunged and held it by the top hinges.

"I kin hold on jest about one more minnit with that dum'd engine puffin' so!" interjected Zero.

But Hensleigh had already jumped into the buggy on the windward side and held the reins with a practiced hand. "I'll take the horse around to the stable and you start on in the coach. You'll take us up on the way. This isn't safe for you. Hurry up! Get in, Zero!"

"Then it isn't safe for you," pleaded Corona, with a quiver in her voice.

"Oh yes, it is, the snow is too deep to hurt, anyway." But he was glad she was troubled about him.

There was a scramble. The boy shot in as from a catapult. There was a prancing and then a dash forward. The buggy lurched, and Corona gave a low cry of fright. But pretty soon the horse, finding its master, settled down to a less dramatic *coup de pied*. As Corona turned to the

Fairharbor coach, now ridiculously low on its unaccustomed runners, it occurred to her that Alexander Hensleigh was just the kind of a man she needed to take care of her.

Mr. Timbers, clad in a tremendous ulster, was stamping his feet impatiently on the porch of the Old Maid's Paradise. The long, easterly swell leaped rhythmically upon the frosted rocks, lapping the snow higher and higher with the tide. At last the stage struggled off the traveled road into the little arc that bounded Corona's cottage. She had left the downs past their autumn brilliancy and soberly taking on their Turkish coloring, like a vast rug, and now they were clothed like a bride in dazzling white.

Zero gave a whoop and landed up to his waist. Mr. Hensleigh drew breath and followed. Mr. Timbers greeted the lady of the house with a curve on his lips as dry as a pine shaving.

"Hev ye got the key?" Like most Fairharbor men, Mr. Timbers spoke very loud.

"I hev, you bet," said Zero proudly.

"I guess we 'd better carry her in; she 'd flounder," suggested the driver. He threw the reins over the horses' backs and stepped off.

"I have always waded through my own drifts," said Corona proudly.

No one of the three men paid the least attention to her remark. At a word from the driver, Mr. Hensleigh stepped forward. The two men picked the woman up. The gentleman's jaw was closed in determination. In the meanwhile Zero and the builder had gone around and unlocked the back door. Mr. Hensleigh did not dare to look at Corona while she put, according to the necessity of the circumstances, her left arm about his neck. But the driver had no such delicacy, for he said: —

"Hold on tight, miss! Don't let your cable slip, or ye 'll be swamped sure."

Obedient to her orders, her left arm increased its pressure, and the widower wondered if her heart beat as violently as his.

The bright day from the front and back doors met in the dining-room. The house was boarded with heavy shutters, and except for this one avenue of light was a cavern of blackness. The cottage, that was as dainty as a lady's work-basket in summer, looked like a dry goods box in winter.

"Ye can't go no further," said Zero at the threshold of the little dining-room. It's up to the rail here." But Mr. Timbers, the builder, swished into the parlor, relying on his rubber boots. Zero hopped after. The driver went back to blanket his horses, and, being well brought up, shut the back door after him. Behind Corona and her lover was a throat of blackness. They seemed to be swallowed up. Before them the front door, opening directly into the parlor, cast a vivid light. The winter sea looked in strangely. The two stood together in the doorway of the dining-room and peered about. The builder and Zero were busily looking around the parlor for leaks. Their heads were turned. Hensleigh was not slow to perceive this. Unconsciously, or perhaps with tenderness prepense, the visitor drew the mistress of the house toward him; while she, in despair over what seemed to her the utter ruin and desolation of her house, suffered his sympathetic caress.

The builder gave a low whistle. "It leaked in over them winders and down the chimbley. I guess I'll hev to tear out them frames. I wasn't calculating on no sich hurricane as this."

"Why doesn't it drain through?" asked Corona, dabbling with the tip of her rubber on the flood that covered the parlor floor. Happily, her straw matting had been taken up when the house was closed.

"This flooring is as tight as if it was caulked," replied the builder proudly. It seemed to him as if it were a great point, that, having taken in water, the house should hold it.

"You seem to have been calculating on its raining from below," said Hensleigh dryly, "or perhaps you expected a tidal wave. Why can't you putty up the seams and put a double coat of paint over? That ought to last and prevent any more leaks," he continued.

"Thet ain't a bad idea. Let me go out and see." The builder went out on the piazza. Of course, Zero followed. What boy wouldn't tag after a mechanic?

The two were left alone for the first time. Corona thought how clever he was to suggest the putty. But he thought, "Now or never."

This time he asked no questions. He simply took the woman in his arms.

"It's no use, Corona," he whispered. "I love you so I can't wait."

"But, Zero!" she fluttered.

Now when a woman thinks more about what people will say than about her own feelings, a man may know that she is not unwilling.

"It sha'n't be called ' Old Maid's Paradise' any longer, if I can help it," he insisted. "When shall we change the name, dear?"

"Not yet. Oh, Alec, not yet, dear!"

"Shall it be the middle of June? Quick!" There was the munching of feet on the furry snow.

"Quick! They are coming!"

"Alec! Don't — yes, then — yes!"

It was all over in that moment. Mr. Timbers returned, tramping heavily. Zero followed, swishing over the wet floor like a school of herring.

The woman, as is usual in an embarrassing position, was the first to recover her self-possession.

"I'll leave the whole thing to you, Mr. Timbers. Do as you please. My rubber leaks, and I'll have to get out of this."

"If ye'd said that before, ye might have saved yer car fare," grunted Mr. Timbers.

"Yes, I might, but if I had" — The lady did not finish her sentence.

CHAPTER II

THE WEDDING

IT was a resplendent morning of the last Saturday of June. Corona awoke and looked around her. Her heart beat as if she were going to her execution at noon; but the sun looked in about the blue and white room as if she were going to Heaven.

She heard heavy steps upon the stairs. The edge of a tray knocked on the door. Puelvir walked in. Puelvir was Corona's nominal cook and practical duenna. If I may inherit the statement of the original documents, Puelvir was Corona's guide, philosopher, and friend. Puelvir's face was as long as the boom of a cup defender, and, far from protecting the cup, she allowed her tears to rain copiously into the coffee. Corona observed this bridal expression with dismay.

"Dear me, Puelvir, what is the matter with you, this morning?"

"I — I wish you jo—boo hoo—oy. Oh, me! Oh, me!" wailed Puelvir. "But I don't wish *him* none," she added viciously.

"Thank you, Puelvir — I am surprised. I thought you would be glad to see me happy."

Puelvir doused a fist into her eyes. "I hain't no ob—bob—jection to seein' *you* happy. But oh, the resk on 't! I darsn't think of that!"

Corona turned pale at this, for her own heart echoed the words.

"Here, take it!" Puelvir plumped the breakfast tray down upon the bed. "It's the last breakfast I'll be bringing yer."

"But, Puelvir!" cried Corona, — "I thought you were going to stay by me. I couldn't live without you."

"I hain't seen any evidence of it. I wish I had n't — oh, boo— hoo— had n't turned off the raspberry man for you! I'd 'a' ben a bride long before you was. Now he's got that widder with four and six of his own into the bargain — and you've ben an' broke our bargain, and here I be!'"

An appalling vision of being deserted by her housemaid on her wedding-day swept over Corona. She saw herself spending her honeymoon frying cunners and teaching Alexander to set the table and wash the dishes. Puelvir stood stern and uncompromising.

"I'll see you through the ceremony, anyhow. I suppose ye won't want to see me nor nobody after that. My trunk's packed. I sot up last night to do it. Why don't ye drink yer coffee?"

The maid looked down upon her mistress. What did she see? Tears gathering in those dear eyes upon their wedding-day. Puelvir's faithful heart melted before the sight like the sugar in the saucer beneath her tears.

"Law, Miss Corona, I won't — there now! I won't, nohow. My trunk ain't packed, neither. That was a whopper. I

would n't be so sneakin' mean. I 'll stick
by you. There 's only one thing," said
Puelvir, swelling grandly: "Don't you ever
ask me to bring his breakfast up to *him*.
I won't do it!"

"Dear me, Puelvir, I don't think Mr.
Hensleigh would ever expect it." Corona
blushed. It seemed to her as if Puelvir
were very indelicate. "He is not at all
spoiled," pleaded the lady.

"He will be soon enough!" snapped the
maid.

Then Puelvir, whether from remorse for
her own cruelty, or from the tenderness of
her own loyalty, took Corona's delicate
hand in her red, work-worn fingers, im-
printed a resounding kiss upon it, and fled
sobbing from the room.

Corona, much agitated, ate her cold
breakfast. When she came to the coffee
she found it noticeably salt.

The door opened and Matthew Launcelot walked in. Matthew was Corona's dog ;
he had acquired a mysterious ability to open

doors, which would have been worth fifty
dollars a week to him in a variety show.
He had practiced on the doors of Paradise,
which, when they did n't stick, would n't
latch. This habit of his had rather disastrous effects upon his mistress during the
period of her betrothal, and as the little
black-and-tan terrier could under no circumstances be taught how to shut a door, Mr.
Hensleigh had formed the habit of putting
chairs against the doors of the parlor when-
ever he paid his respects to Corona.

Matthew and Corona passed each other
in the middle of the floor. The one leaped
upon the bed, the other shut the door.
(This rhythmical remark may be pardoned
to the general agitation of the wedding-day,
which overpowers even its historian.) Matthew was in the habit of having his breakfast upstairs with his mistress; he finished
off the rolls, begged in vain for the chops,
and called for his usual cup of coffee.

Corona, as she gave it to him, patted the
dog rather wistfully. "You won't desert

me, will you, dear?" The dog looked up
into her face and shook his head. He was
thinking that something was not just right
that morning with the coffee. Corona was
much comforted, for she had the feeling
that she was parting from all her old friends.

Tom and Susy objected on general prin-
ciples to Corona's getting married, but in
particular to Corona's being married in
Fairharbor. Tom, Susy, and the baby were
occupying Corona's only guest room. This
room was painted green. Susy averred that
this color represented the mental status of
the family at that particular time. She
never knew decent people before who refused to be married from their own home.

"But this *is* my home," Corona had
argued; and Tom had said, "Let the girl
do as she wants, and charge the bills to
me."

Mary Sinuous, an old friend of Corona's
maiden days, had torn herself away from
her husband in Brooklyn long enough to
come to the wedding, and to spend one

sleepless night upon the sofa in the parlor. Mary had added to the interest of the last night before Corona's wedding by tumbling off the sofa three times. Perhaps the sofa was a little narrow and somewhat slanting. It had been courted on a good deal during the last few weeks, and the springs were not at their best. And every time that Mary fell, Matthew Launcelot, who had experience with burglars, set up an ungodly barking. This made the baby cry, and Tom say things that percolated through the matched-board cottage. Take it all in all, it was not a comfortable night, and the family was glad to get up.

The wedding was appointed at one o'clock. The widower's brother, a clergyman of a celibate disposition, but of undoubted family loyalty, came from a flourishing parish in a distant part of the State to perform the ceremony. These two stayed at the hotel, and presented themselves at intervals with a shamefaced consciousness of inferiority which is characteristic of the masculine gender at such a time. The widower was seen that morning by the neighbors aimlessly taking trips to and fro on the Fairharbor ferry, and looking as pale as a new mainsail. His brother, from time to time, would slap him vigorously upon the back.

"Heavens, Alec, cheer up!" he would say. "You ought to be used to it by this time. Now if it were I" — But the jocoseness of the clerical gentleman fell as flat as a sinker, and he perceived that it is not good form even for a brother to remind a man of his first wedding-day upon the morning of his second.

But Corona had no other wedding-day to think of. And Susy thought of the guests, while Tom managed the caterer. That colored gentleman had arrived from a distinguished firm in Boston on the early train, and took immediate possession of the house. Consequently, such of the family as were not favored with breakfast in their bedrooms had to eat it where they could. It should be remembered that the main house was only twenty feet cube. Tom ate his chops on the hogshead cover by the back door. While he was doing this the caterer approached with a face as nearly pale as is possible to a frightened African.

"I declare, sir, they have forgotten the patties. What shall I do?"

"What kind of patties?"

"Chicken, sir."

"Then telegraph immediately to have them sent right out on the 10.45 by a special messenger. I never heard of a wedding without patties. Have you?" sternly.

"No," replied the bewildered caterer, "I never have, sir."

"I don't believe the ceremony would be legal," replied Tom authoritatively. "I cannot have my sister married without patties."

The caterer was working miracles in the little toy house. The dining-room was nine feet by ten. The caterer had the delicacy not to intimate that this was not a spacious

apartment.　He made it look ninety by a
hundred.

Puelvir eyed the caterer with scorching
distrust, and told him she supposed her
silver and doilies were not good enough for
him.　Matthew Launcelot, on the contrary,
took a fancy to the caterer.　How far this
could be explained by the disappearance of
a lobster croquette and two macaroons has
never been accurately determined.

And now the guests began to arrive.
They were not very many.　They might
have been hundreds, but they were com-
prised almost within the first ten numerals.
This surprising limitation was purely a
matter of mathematics.　The parlor of Paradise could not prettily hold more than a
dozen people, and Corona would be married
in that parlor.

Mrs. Rowin, Zero's mother, came first.
Corona had sent Zero for her with The
Lady of Shalott and the buggy.　The Lady
of Shalott was then tied to the clothes-post,
so that no member of the family might be

absent from the ceremony. Corona requested that the window be open, so that
The Lady could look in. Zero followed in
his best clothes. He calmly took up his
position under the canopy of Cape Ann
roses especially prepared for the bride.
Tom marched him out of it and deposited
him behind the stove, where Zero stood up
straight against the wall and upset twenty-
four bride's roses and a vase on a bracket
that hung too low.

An old friend of the bride's, known to
prehistoric tradition as Effie, drove over
from Wolchester with a span, and reflected
a pale glory of the world which just saved
the occasion.

Father Morrison, otherwise known as the
lobster man, to Susy's silent despair and
Puelvir's audible disgust, had received
cards for the wedding; but Effie had met
him at a housewarming in the cottage some
years ago, and asked him to sit by her side
upon the sofa. Father Morrison felt that
he was the guest of honor.

It was a solemn question what to do with
Matthew Launcelot. Corona wanted him
present, but Alexander, who was not a
favorite with the terrier, dryly suggested
that he did n't care to be snapped at while
he was putting the ring on, and advised
that the dog be sequestered.

"I won't have the critter in the kitchen
on a day like this," said Puelvir sternly.
"The hogshead is covered. Tie him up
atop on 't. He 'll set there very comfortable."

Corona had secret doubts on the subject.
But Tom drove a nail up, fastened one end
of a rope to it, and the other to the dog's
collar, and Matthew Launcelot sullenly accepted this obloquy.

But Corona lingered upstairs in her room
as long as she could. She felt as if she
might never again be alone. She wished
she had a mother, before whom she could
kneel at this supreme moment, and of whose
blessing she could be sure! But thoughts
like these bring tears, and tears must not
come now.

Corona threw up the shade, and then opened the window. She did not know it, but she had looked before this like a white ghost. Now the sun touched her with color, and made her human. Before her the bay glittered in the soft breeze. The water looked like ruffled velvet. The expanse that once typified the limitless to her mind, seemed contracted beside the vastness that the happy future spread before her imagination. She turned away. She could not bear the sea at that moment.

Her eyes fell upon her favorite books. There was the Bible which she read every night. There was her inseparable Robertson. There was her dearest Tennyson and her Shakespeare in ten blue volumes, to match the room. She crossed over and took up her Bible and patted it, and then with an impulsive movement put her cheek against its worn cover. "Dear, dear little room!" she thought. "No matter what the future is, no one can take me away from these old friends."

Her sister-in-law had said to her one day,
"Have you thought, Co, what it is going to
mean to give up your freedom?" As Susy
quecned it utterly over Tom and over the
whole family, this remark had not struck
Corona as one of those aphorisms which are
born of experience. But now it came back
to her. Give up her freedom — everything?
Yes! ten thousand times!"

"Coro! Coro!" Susy's positive voice,
softened into a ceremonious whisper, rever-
berated up the stairs. The bride started.
She forgot to look in the mirror, or she
would have seen that her cheeks were as
white as her wedding dress. Her time had
come! She opened the door. There was
a whisk of retreating petticoats, and on the
landing, quite by himself, stood Alexander
the Conqueror. The man swept his beautiful bride with one swift glance. Then an
expression of reverence and humility settled
upon his face.

.   .   .   .

They walked into their own parlor without ushers or bridesmaids. The front door, leading directly into the room, was open. The minister faced them solemnly. The sea looked in, like an uninvited guest, that loved the bride too much to stay away.

Puelvir, dressed in black alpaca, with jet bracelets and lace mitts, and weeping profusely, followed her mistress. The caterer stood in the dining-room door.

Tom looked from guest to guest about the room, and then glanced apprehensively at his wife. These natural protectors of the bride had made a fearful discovery — there were thirteen in the room! Should they speak about it, or not? But Corona and Tom always understood each other without talking. Her quick eye had taken it all in.

"Get in Matthew Launcelot! He 'll make fourteen," she whispered to her brother. But Susy received this proposition with scorn. Meanwhile the minister, with the indifference of his class to heathen superstitions, had noticed nothing. He had a beautiful marriage ceremony of his own, and before anybody realized it he had begun to read it with a deep voice. Tom, who had actually started for the dog, was arrested halfway to the door. The Rev. Mr. Hensleigh's preliminary selection of Scripture verses was dignified and impressive. Upon every face in the room there had already settled a serious look. The groom, with trembling fingers, was taking the wedding-ring out of his waistcoat pocket. The bride's heart was tempestuously beating, "I will, I will, I will." Could she say it so that anybody could hear?

At that moment the sound of cowhide boots thundered over the piazza and drowned the clergyman's tones.

"Hullo!" cried a husky voice, "here's them patties from Boston, Miss Corona, and I want forty cents for bringin' of 'em over on a special trip!" Alas, it was the local expressman, to whom the caterer's messenger had ignominiously delegated his sacred duty.

The bride's lips twitched. How dreadful if she should laugh! The minister blushed. An awful hush interrupted that wedding ceremony. Tears of mortification sprang to Susy's eyes. "This comes," she thought, "of being married in a clam shell." But Tom was equal to the occasion. This man of the world marched up to the expressman and took him by the collar and shook him.

"At peril of your life," he muttered, "don't you speak again until you're spoken to! Stand just where you are, and take off your hat!" Tom came back into the parlor serenely. "He makes fourteen," he said aloud; "let him be."

The embarrassed minister began over again. The expressman carefully deposited the chicken patties in his hat, and stood with his mouth open. The ceremony proceeded bravely. He willed and she willed; the ring was on and they were one. Corona looked very sweet and happy. Why did everybody cry?

The minister's grave voice ceased. A delicate spell lay over that unworldly wedding. The caterer's eyes were large. "The prettiest I ever saw," he whispered to Puelvir. Nobody else had spoken.

It now becomes my painful duty to record that sharp upon this sacred silence a fearful shriek uprose. This was followed by a spluttering and gurgling such as only the throat of the drowning could emit.

"It's Matthew Launcelot! Run, Puelvir!" These were the first audible words uttered by Corona in the capacity of a married woman.

Puelvir ran. She left the doors all open. "It's him in the hogshead!" she called back at the top of her lungs. "The critter's drownin'! He's sunk the third time!"

The dog, outraged at being shut out from the bosom of his family on such an important occasion, had overturned the cover of the hogshead and had slipped in. Hanging by his rope, he was, in truth, drowning as fast as he conveniently could. Puelvir

hauled him out as if he had been a rock
cod, untied him, cuffed him ou both ears,
and let him go.   Matthew Launcelot made
one dive for the bridal company.   He was
careful not to rid himself of any superflu-
ous water until he got into the parlor, when
he shook himself vigorously all over Susy.
Then he ran right up to the bride.   She
stooped to comfort him.   The dog put his
wet arms around Corona's neck, and she
allowed him.   Thus all the family were
present at the wedding.

"What are you waiting here for?" said
Tom to the expressman half an hour after.

"Them forty cents," replied the expressman sadly.   "I would n't 'a' waited, only
she told me I must never run up a bill.   I
wish her joy, anyhow."

Corona instinctively felt for her pocket-
book in her wedding dress.   But Alexander
Hensleigh, with a grand air of possession,
took out a two-dollar bill and handed it to
the expressman.

"This lady's bills are mine now," he said
with a new face.

"I always like to be among good folks," spoke up Father Morrison at this crisis; "misery loves company."

But the bride gave her husband a beautiful look. She felt as if no one could notice it, and he hoped that no one did.

Then, when Tom came up and offered her a chicken patty, and called her "Mrs. Hensleigh," she understood that she was a married woman.

CHAPTER III

THE WEDDING JOURNEY

THE coach had carried off the wedding guests. Only Zero and Father Morrison were left.

"I wish ye a pleasant trip," said the lobster man, dipping his head like a Cape boat in a ground swell. Father Morrison meant "trip" in the nautical sense, like a trip to the Grand Banks. But the bride laughed gayly as she thanked her old neighbor. She understood the word in the marriage sense.

"I suppose ye 'll be back in time for herrin'," added the old man. "I 'd rather be miser'ble in good company than happy in bad." Corona hardly knew whether to take this as a prophecy of ill fortune or not. But Father Morrison, feeling that he had given the couple his best benediction, hobbled up the path to his little home.

Corona and Alexander had at least one conviction in common. Neither of them believed in the old shoe and the rice business as a necessary conclusion of the wedding ceremony.

"It is undignified," said Corona sententiously.

"It is dangerous," echoed Alexander scientifically. "I once knew a fellow to have a piece of rice lodge in his ear. It was the year before " —

"How dreadful, Alec! It did n't " —

"Yes, it did. He became deaf, and all his wife's scolding was lost upon him."

"And all her dearness, too," Corona answered, with a happy look. So it had been decided to reverse the usual order of things.

"The rest can take the 4.10 train, and we can follow on the 5.03, if we must have a wedding trip, Alec; and we will drive over with The Lady of Shalott and send the baggage ahead by the coach." Thus the lady decided the matter. But further she would take no responsibility. In her heart of hearts she wanted to spend her honeymoon in Paradise, by the great waters, in her own dear home. But her husband could not understand the simplicity of such a wish. He mentioned Niagara; followed this fossil bridal suggestion by a casual hint about Alaska; threw out ominous insinuations about San Francisco, Mexico, and New Orleans, and ended by a bold plea for a yachting trip to Cape Breton. Corona's heart was faint at the suggestion of these endless wanderings, and she utterly refused to be told what his plans were. She made only one condition: that he should buy no long-distance tickets in advance.

Zero stood at The Lady's head. He was to take the ferry over to the station and bring the horse back. His face, usually stolid with the inherited woe of generations of fisher folk, was now expanded to its uttermost expression. Zero wore the smiles of a lifetime; for the chance of a lifetime had been his. Croquettes and patties, ice cream and cake left over, fruits and coffee and candies had contributed in fabulous quantities to his ecstatic condition. Zero could not have run to a fire; but he had known one day of perfect bliss, and that is more than many wiser than Zero can say.

Puelvir, with Matthew Launcelot tied to a string, stood upon the little piazza sobbing.   •

"Are you sure you have got everything?" Alexander turned to his bride with the caution of an old traveler. "We may not be back for a long time; possibly not for a month."

"Perhaps it won't be more than two weeks, dear. How can you leave such a lovely spot? Look out there!" Corona shaded her eyes and glanced out upon the sea. The sun gleamed over the western coast. The whistling buoy moaned faintly from around the Point, as if protesting against her departure. Even then the originality and the comfort of not doing exactly what all married couples do did not dawn upon the man's mind. It had always been a wonder to Corona that newly-wedded couples did not absolutely loathe each other after the regulation journey — the nauseating travel, the buffet food, the vulgar hotel. "What a horrible way of beginning life together!" she thought; and now her turn had come, and where were all her ideals? Alexander did not answer, but Matthew did, while Puelvir — as if it were the dog who was crying — jerked him up violently by the string.

"You'll be very careful of him," said Corona. "Don't let him out without watching, and always lead him when you go to walk; and look out for the house. You had better stay right here, as we may be back any day. We will telegraph in plenty of time." Corona was used to managing, and this was her house, and Puelvir was hers.

"I'll sot right at the kitchen winder 'n' watch for that Christian Union Telegraph boy," wailed Puelvir, "for I sha'n't hev nothin' else to do 'thout it's runnin' after this here critter. What 'll I do if he breaks away on me to foller after yer? He 's capable on't."

"At last!" said Hensleigh exultingly, as he placed his bride in the buggy, and took the reins. Corona looked back. There stood her own plain Paradise, and there stood her faithful Puelvir convulsively waving a flopping handkerchief — and there was Matthew Launcelot yapping out his broken black-and-tan heart. It seemed to Corona, and her eyes grew suddenly moist, that she had left the whole world behind. Then she turned to her husband. A new world lay before her. The bride brushed his shoulder with her cheek. He answered her not in words. From that moment he could have taken her into the furthest wilderness, for Paradise was with him.

When they reached the station Corona noticed that she was the centre of observation. This annoyed her exceedingly; she had never been a bride before.

"It 's this new traveling-dress," she said.

"I ought to have had my own way and worn an old one." She glanced down at the pretty dove-colored cloth skirt. "I'll go and check the baggage, Alec," she said with a burning face, "while you are getting the tickets." The instinct of many independent years looked out of the bride's eyes; but the instinct of generations of masculine supremacy replied from the eyes of the groom.

"You stay just where you are," he said quietly; "I am fully capable of checking my wife's baggage in addition to my own."

"Oh," said Corona, "I never thought of that! You see I have taken care of myself a good while."

"You must learn to be taken care of now," her husband said.

It was with a feeling of mingled anxiety and relief that Corona settled back into her seat. The car was warm, and Alexander devotedly helped her off with her pretty jacket and hung it upon the rack. The train moved off slowly, and Corona looked out of the southern window, dreamily watching for the last view of the harbor and her little home.

At that moment there was a shriek at the upper end of the car, and an extraordinary commotion seemed to have set in among the passengers. The brakeman was in violent altercation with somebody.

" Here, you ! Stop there! Hi! Catch him! Get off! You've no business aboard!"

"It 's one of the Fairharbor drunkards. Poor fellow!" sighed Corona.

"Mad dog!" came the startling cry. Everybody jumped to his feet. Hensleigh threw himself in an attitude of protection before his wife. A black shadow scurried down the aisle. This was followed by a beardless brakeman and the conductor of the white mustache. Past the terrified passengers, skillfully eluding his pursuers, darting under the arms of the infuriated husband, a little black-and-tan figure leaped — sprang upon the bride, all over her beautiful dress, and laid his head upon her deli-

cate silk blouse. It was Matthew Launcelot.

"The d—— dog!" said Hensleigh set-
tling back with a groan.

"You dear thing!" cried Corona, unty-
ing the piece of chewed-off rope from the
terrier's collar. "What a hard time you 've
had! How glad I am to see you!"

"I 'm not," said Hensleigh brutally, "I
wish he were in — at — home!"

"So he 's yours, Miss" — said the conductor, nodding to his well-remembered
passenger.

"This is Mrs. Hensleigh," interrupted
Alexander with an air of great offense.

"Beg pardon," said the conductor. "I
wish you well, I 'm sure; it is n't usual to
take 'em on such trips. Some of the passengers got the idea he 's mad."

"I can heave him over the Cut!" cried
the brakeman.

"You 'll heave me over too!" flashed
Corona. She clasped Matthew Launcelot
firmly to her heart.

"Put him off!" came a shout from the other end of the car. Now the object of all this commotion was quite indifferent to it, but busily divided his time between kissing his mistress and snarling at Mr. Hensleigh and the brakeman.

"This is unbearable!" muttered Alexander between his teeth. "No hotel in the land would take a dog like this!"

"It is too bad," said Corona soothingly. "What shall we do? Of course, we can't travel with him."

"Perhaps they 'll take him in at Barker's. I know them pretty well, and we can send him back by express to-morrow."

"By no means!" cried Corona. "They put them in dungeons down in the basement. Matthew would die, and you *know* he can't bear an expressman. I don't see any way but that we 'll have to get off at West Fairharbor and take him home."

"Well," sighed the bridegroom patiently, "it 's asking a good deal of a fellow; but I suppose we can take the late train."

"Here you are, then!" cried the brakeman.

"I'm very sorry," said the conductor.

An audible sigh of relief arose from the passengers as this bridal party prepared to leave the train. Hensleigh's expression was a cross between humiliation and fury. But Corona and Matthew Launcelot looked perfectly contented.

The only inhabitant of West Fairharbor seemed to be the station-master, who regarded the wedding party sternly. Corona, forgetting that she had a husband, marched up to the man and confidingly said: —

"I suppose the next train will take us back in half an hour?"

"None don't stop here fur two hours, mum; I've got to go home to supper," was the grim reply; and deigning to take no further notice of the passengers, the agent locked the station and lounged away. Corona and Alexander looked at each other, and then at Matthew Launcelot.

"I should think you might know your

own country," began Hensleigh impatiently, and then stopped, biting his lip, for he remembered that he was a bridegroom.

"I 'm sorry," said Corona humbly.   She bent over and kissed Matthew, as if that helped the matter.   She dropped upon the baggage truck, looking very much troubled.

Before her an inlet of the harbor began to be gilded in the setting sun.   It was a tortuous stream that connected two bays, and which made an island of Fairharbor and the Cape.   Great stretches of marsh were disappearing before the rising tide. Green hummocks were nodding their hair for the last time before they went under for the night.   Near the station was an inlet to an inlet; but the harbor was out of sight three miles and more away to the south.

"I suppose we can camp here," said Alexander grimly.   "This truck, a settee, and a flour barrel are about all the assets of the situation.   The flour barrel seems to be empty, and to save any further complications I move we put the dog in there and head him up."

But Matthew Launcelot was not so easily to be disposed of. He had brought them into this predicament; he had spoiled the wedding journey. The position was indeed a serious one. But it was Matthew's good luck to bring them out. He began to bark furiously, and ran down through a pine grove toward the shore. Corona followed, and her husband, with a sardonic expression of the features, brought up the rear leisurely. The bridal procession arrived at the beach. Hensleigh suggested that all that was needed was a band, and began to whistle a few bars from "Lohengrin."

But Matthew had made a momentous discovery. It was nothing less than a man and a dory.

"Stop!" cried Corona. "Where are you going?"

"I'm goin' to Twenty Poun' Island as soon as I can shove her off."

Hensleigh opened his mouth to speak, but Corona went on with beautiful unconsciousness: —

"Won't you take us? There are only three — I mean two."

The fisherman looked at the group suspiciously, and grudgingly said: —

"Well, I mought, if ye'll leave the dog behind."

"Sensible man!" This was Hensleigh's first chance to speak, and he made the most of it. Then, gently putting his wife to one side, he closed a whispered bargain with the owner of the dory.

"He won't take us any further than the Island, and only on condition that you put the dog in the stern locker and sit on him," explained Hensleigh. "And how in thunder are we to get home from there?"

"Oh, delightful!" cried Corona. "Why, I know *every* fisherman in the harbor, and any of them will take us over. They'll be just coming home from their traps."

"I'd rather they wouldn't all see us," suggested Alexander, helping his wife in from the sedgy bank; "I do hope it won't get out in the papers."

The bride and groom sat on the thwart together. Except for the rising of the tide, and for the eddying currents, the water was motionless. They might just as well have been alone, for the fisherman rowed with his body half and his head wholly turned away. He was not thinking of his passengers. He was intent upon the straightest channel.

And now the outline of the western hills grew purple and black, and now a hundred windows of the city ahead reflected the departing glory of the sun with a brilliance that dazzled and elated at once. Then a turn in the channel, and the passengers in the dory were face to face with the gorgeous tints that the clouds above the setting sun threw upon the vitreous surface of the motionless water. Peace rested upon sea and land. Even the dog was awed into silence. All the irritation and disappointment were fanned away from the hearts of these two people who loved each other better than all the world. They sat together — with hands clasped — not talking, looking into each other's eyes, and into the face of the purple horizon. It occurred to Corona that this bridal trip was typical of the married life before her: plenty of little things moving in the current with the big ones — little troubles, little disappointments, little frets, but all borne — how easily! — upon the great sea of love. They were startled by the grating of the keel.

"Here you are! Out with you!" The fisherman held his dory firmly with his oar.

There was another dory pulled up on the beach. It was an old black boat with a green streak.

"Why, that's Father Morrison!" observed Corona suddenly. "He's leaving lobsters at the lighthouse."

"Thank God!" said Hensleigh devoutly. "I begin to see my way clear for the first time since we have started on our wedding journey. I believe we can catch the nine o'clock train, after all."

Corona made no reply.

Father Morrison came down from the lighthouse, and with the serenity of his class, accepted the appearance of the bride and groom stranded on Twenty Pound Island with an unpopular dog as a matter of course. He took them aboard his lobster boat. By this time the bride's traveling-dress was so far on the road to ruin that she looked upon the lobsters in the bottom of the boat with indifference. It was now growing dusk. Hensleigh, spying a dry spot, tried to sit in the bow, but Father Morrison waved him sternly back: —

"You go set along side o' her. That's where you belong." Hensleigh meekly obeyed, for a captain is master, even in a lobster dory.

The old man rowed them strongly out into the harbor. He pulled his ash oars with the might that old age allows only to fisher folk. It was darkening fast. The square-cut lines of Paradise grew nearer and fainter at the same time. There was a light in the kitchen window, and Corona thought that she could detect figures on the piazza.

Father Morrison rested on his oars, and with an oratorical cough raised himself to his feet.

"I wish ye," he began solemnly, "fair winds and a pleasant harbor."

Hensleigh took off his hat, and said, "Amen!"

"Thank you, dear Father Morrison," echoed Corona softly.

But, as usual, Matthew Launcelot had the last word. A fearful howl arose from between the rower's feet. The dog leaped into Corona's lap. A live, green lobster followed.

"He's got him by the leg!" cried Corona. "Father Morrison, he'll kill him."

"There! There!" said Father Morrison, "I'll see to him," and he wrenched the jaws of the lobster asunder as if they had been a clothes-pin. Matthew, with a yell of agony, leaped into the water and swam ashore. The boat grated on the rocks.

As the bridal couple clambered up the cliff, they were met by Puelvir, Zero, the expressman, and a policeman.

"Mercy on us!" cried Puelvir. "It's him! It's him! I've had the whole town huntin' after the critter — And Lord have mercy on us, it's *them!*"

"You can go, and I'm much obleeged," said Puelvir loftily to the expressman and policeman. "My folks have got home, and I don't need any more of you. The critter's here!"

If there were a trifling ambiguity in Puelvir's last substantive, nobody noticed it. But Corona leaned dependently upon her husband's arm for the first time since they had been married.

"I'm so glad to get home," she said, "are n't you? And, Puelvir, dear, could n't you get us a little supper?"

They sat on the piazza to rest; Puelvir in the kitchen was singing a joyous alto. She sang: —

"Safe, safe at home,
No more to roam;
Safe, safe at home."

The odor of a delicious supper — plainly one of Puelvir's masterpieces — crept around the side of the house.

The stars came out, and the harbor lanterns laughed across the bay. And then the red flash-light from the Point turned its greeting eye and welcomed them. Everything seemed to have expected them. Corona was very happy.

"It wasn't such a bad wedding trip, after all, was it, dear?" she ventured.

"N-no-o," doubtfully answered honest Alexander. He was still thinking of Niagara, Mexico, Alaska, Cape Breton, and the nine o'clock train.

"Isn't this better than a hot, stuffy hotel?" pleaded Corona again, her sweet breath fanning his beard.

And now a cool wave of salt air swept over Paradise, and the waves sang on the rocks at their feet. The supper bell rang.

"I don't know but you are right, dear," said Hensleigh, with a sigh of content. Hand in hand the two went in and closed the door.

CHAPTER IV

THE FIRST MISUNDERSTANDING

ALEXANDER was fishing for cunners, — an exciting occupation with which he dignified his honeymoon. He dangled his legs over the edge of the cliff, lazily smoking a briarwood. His straw hat was tipped back from his forehead, and he was watching with a fisherman's intentness the tidal eddy beneath him. Corona sat by his side making believe that she was very happy. In point of fact, there was nothing she hated so much as fishing in the hot sun. But the three weeks' wife had already learned that happiness consisted in doing what Alexander liked. Hensleigh, who knew next to nothing about the natural history of the Fairharbor cunner, insisted that they never bit before twelve o'clock.

"I have never noticed that they bit at

all," said Corona, "and I have lived here four summers." The bride looked cool and beautiful in her white flannel boating-dress, as she happily jeered at her husband's efforts.

But Alexander did not answer. He gave his wife a debonair glance. The last bite had taken his bait. With a swish of jaunty superiority he brought his line in and sacrificed another rock snail.

These two people were as happy as they looked. Hensleigh had grown ten years younger. It was the lover of the old days come back. And Corona — ah, but Corona! Who can put into words that ineffable glory which looks from the eyes of a rapturous, new-made wife? She was like a rose just burst into bloom. When marriage overtakes people past the first enthusiasm of youth they are apt to be happier than younger people know how to be. Happiness is a fine art which only experience can teach us how to acquire. Most of us dabble at it. A few master it.

Fairharbor was nothing if not accommodating. It was one of the pleasant peculiarities of that place that the United States mail was delivered on the rocks and beaches. Corona's particular letter-carrier was very devoted to her. On one occasion, while she was taking a surf bath, he was courteous enough to deliver her letters to her in the water. He was late this morning, and did not go up to the house, but took a short cut across the rocks to them, and hurried by. Hensleigh did not even look up. He had refused since he had been married even to read the morning papers. He went on contentedly trying to murder fish, while Corona read her letters and his own too.

He was suddenly diverted from his ecstatic occupation by a long sigh.

"Oh, dear," cried Corona, "it's too bad!"

"What's the matter, dear?"

"Why, I've got to go in to Boston."

Hensleigh's lips fairly turned pale. He dropped his pole. "*In to Boston!*" he exclaimed. If she had said Calcutta he could not have thrown more emphasis into these two words — such a change had Paradise wrought upon the nature of the erstwhile traveling bridegroom. "Why, Corona! When I magnanimously gave up Alaska, Niagara, Cape Breton, and Mexico, I did n't expect to be yanked out of my home to go to — *Boston!*"

"Oh, but *you* have n't got to go," said Corona sweetly. "I can attend to it myself. I always have."

"Do you mean to say that you would go off and leave me here alone — with — with Matthew Launcelot, and we not yet married four weeks?" demanded the husband with a real constraint.

"Why, Alec, love, I don't see of what possible use you can be. It 's about the insurance. It has been overdue two weeks, and just because I was married I forgot all about it."

"You sound," observed her husband dryly, "as if you wish you had n't been.

And it does n't seem to occur to you that, having taken a husband, it is natural for him to look out for your business affairs. I *have* insured property before in my life." He stood up, viciously flung out his line, and immediately landed a sculpin.

Corona screamed — a feminine, horror-stricken shriek. Matthew Launcelot, hearing the commotion, ran out of the house to defend his mistress. Perceiving the sculpin, he turned his undivided attention to that subject.

Hensleigh, with a look of unutterable disgust, threw down his pole and stalked into the house. Corona looked after him in genuine astonishment. She felt suddenly very faint. What did this mean? What had she done? Only three weeks married, and he turned his back upon her! There was nothing else for the woman to do. She followed him anxiously.

When she came in she found him in the parlor officiously reading "Les Miserables." It was a big, red, aggressive-looking copy, and he put it down with some noise when she entered.

"Alec, dear" — she began.

"What train do you take?" he interrupted austerely.

"I — I don't know," she trembled. "The agent says it must be attended to right away, and I thought I might find Tom" —

"Tom!" exploded the husband. "What in the world do you want of Tom?"

"I don't know," faltered Corona. "I thought — he always has" — She broke off, confused beneath her husband's steady glance.

"Do you think, Corona, that your husband is capable of doing an elemental piece of business or not? Is he to be of ornament, or of use? We might as well have it settled right now."

Corona looked frightened.

"I did n't mean" — she said. "I 've always done these things. I like to do them, too," she added in a stronger voice. "I enjoy looking out for myself."

"Does it ever occur to you that I might enjoy looking out for you?" Hensleigh got up and gazed out of the window. "Besides," he added, "a man has some feeling on such a subject."

Corona stared at him, puzzled. So had she some feeling about it. When a man's traditions and a woman's independence come in contact, what is to be done?

Alexander sat down at his table and began to write.

"How long did your policy run?" he inquired in a methodical voice.

"Three years."

"What premium?"

Now Corona never in her life had been able to remember what was the premium and which was the policy. She would have died rather than let Alexander know this just then.

"Let me see," she returned evasively. "The house cost me five hundred dollars; the furniture, one hundred. House, furniture, clothes, and all — I insured them for six hundred and fifty."

"What is the company?" came the cool rejoinder.

"The Mutual Frying Pan and Fire Insurance Company. It's in the same building, you remember, with my brokers, Jump & Jiggles."

By the time she had finished her explanation, Hensleigh began to read her the following letter: —

GENERAL AGENT MUTUAL FRYING PAN AND FIRE INS. CO. : —

Sir: In reply to yours of the —— inst. addressed to my wife, Mrs. Corona Hensleigh, I inclose my check for amount due you for a renewal of policy for a term of three years. Hold insurance from receipt of this, and forward policy at your earliest convenience to

Yours truly,
ALEXANDER HENSLEIGH.

"There," he said, "that's all that's necessary to do."

"But I always *have* gone to Boston," insisted Corona pugnaciously.

"You have n't always been married, though."

There was something a little peremptory in Hensleigh's tone, which jarred upon his wife. A man never understands why a woman resents masterfulness at one time and likes it at another. If a tramp had come in and frightened her, and Alexander had kicked him into the harbor, she would have adored this evidence of power. But the superior and patronizing manner with which her husband drew that check was another matter. Corona did not like it, and she showed that she did not.

"Very well," she said coldly. "If you don't wish me to go I certainly shall not."

"Do as you please," he replied shortly. He took up " Les Miserables," and with an air of great significance he fastened his eyes upon the title.

Corona turned sadly away. She went out on the piazza and looked at the harbor for comfort. A cloud had swept over the hot, noon sky, and the water regarded her darkly. She called Matthew Launcelot. This member of the family came up dragging the mutilated sculpin, which he proceeded to bury in the folds of her white dress. With an exclamation of annoyance Corona fled to the kitchen. Puelvir was ironing one of Alexander's outing - shirts, and her temper and the thermometer stood at about a hundred and sixteen.

"This ain't no place fur you," began Puelvir sharply. "You 'd better go to *him*. I ain't no time to be stirrin' up desserts fur him to-day. You send him out berryin'. It 's about all he 's good fur."

Corona retreated in despair. There was no one left but her husband. She went through the dining-room, where she had received her first kiss, and, as she advanced, her heart grew warmer. She softly opened the parlor door. He did not look up from his book. Nevertheless, Corona was convinced that he had not been reading. She stole up behind him, put her arms about his neck, and looked over his shoulder. "Les Miserables" was upside down.

"Let me have the letter, dear. I'll run out and mail it. I won't go to Boston. I don't think there is any real need of it."

"Oh, come here!" cried Alexander rapturously. "Les Miserables" performed a double somersault and landed upon the piazza. Matthew Launcelot took the red book to be another kind of sculpin, and began viciously to tear it to pieces. And the bride — where was she?

.   .   .   .

In a few minutes two figures stole out of Paradise, hand in hand. Alexander carried a little Indian basket, and Corona carried the letter. When the dinner-bell called them home their eyes eagerly told each other that they had brought back something sweeter than the wild strawberries which were offered to Puelvir as an ironing-day dessert.

The day passed pleasantly. Corona and

Alexander were very happy. After supper, as usual, Hensleigh lighted a cigar. It had come up a little easterly and threatened rain, and after a few ineffectual attempts to stay on the piazza, Alexander came into the house. Corona, who was sitting at the window, greeted him joyously. But when she saw his cigar her bright face fell.

"Why, Alec, dear, you're not smoking, are you — to-night?"

"Great Scott! child, why in thunder shouldn't I smoke to-night?"

"Why, don't you remember — the insurance?"

"Well, what about the insurance? I thought we had settled that little matter."

"But, my dear, it's overdue."

"Over — fiddlesticks!" exclaimed Hensleigh with a little, contemptuous smile.

"Don't be rude." Corona arose with some dignity.

"I won't," he replied quickly, "if you're not silly." She flushed at the word.

"But don't you see, if the house burns down to-night, I sha'n't get a cent for it?"

"So?" he said, puffing peacefully. His equanimity and her anxiety stung Corona.

"Let me see," he said quietly, dropping his ashes on the floor, "this insurance has been two weeks overdue, and I have smoked every day in this house. I do not see any reason why I should give it up now."

"I see every reason," she said severely. "I did n't *know* it before. It would break my heart to lose this house. I love it very dearly."

"You love it more than you do me," observed the husband chillingly.

"No," she returned, "I love it more than I do your tobacco."

In a quiet, aggravating way Hensleigh kept on smoking. He looked at her cheerfully, as much as to say, "Poor girl, you 're cracked a little on the subject, and I 'm sorry for you." Corona stood for a moment in anxious thought, and then with set lips walked up to his chair and stood over him.

"Are you going to keep on smoking, Alec?"

"So it seems, my dear."

"I must beg you — I must ask you, not to do it until the new policy is taken out. It is n't safe. It 's *very* dangerous."

Hensleigh looked up at his wife quizzically.

"Whose house is this?" he asked.

"Why, mine!" said Corona.

"Ah! I thought it was ours." Without another word Hensleigh went out, shut the door, stood for a moment irresolute on the piazza, and then disappeared in the growing darkness. His feet crunched on the crisp grass. There had been a three weeks' Fairharbor drought, and everything was very dry.

Corona dropped on the sofa, stunned. Oh, what had happened? Where had he gone? Would he ever come back? It seemed to the bride as if her husband had gone out of her life forever. Too proud to follow him, too heartbroken to stay behind, she wandered out wretchedly and uncertainly upon the rocks. The wind was ris-

ing, and the incoming tide dashed high.
She put up her hands and found her cheeks
wet. "It's the spray," she thought. But
it was not the spray.

She could no longer hide her feeling
from herself. She threw herself down upon
the rock and cried as if she would cry her
life out. Not fifty feet away sat her husband, smoking desperately. The wind carried the smoke the other way. The cliff
towered between the two. It might have
been the width of the world.

Suddenly shrill sounds came from the
house. Neither of these two miserable people paid any attention to them. It was
only Matthew. Perhaps the expressman
had come. But human shrieks now broke
into the canine outcries. Puelvir began to
call frantically.

"Fire! Fire! Miss Corona, yer house
is afire!" It didn't occur to Puelvir to
call the master of the house.

Simultaneously with these words the
smell of something burning rushed over the

rocks. Corona ran; but Hensleigh ran, too; and he got there first.

"Paradise is *afire!*" cried Puelvir. "Somebody 's sot it. The piazza 's burnin' up!" She was vigorously emptying the contents of the parlor flower vases upon the fire. Hensleigh stooped and looked. A horrible conviction forced itself upon him that a spark from his cigar had started the dry grass into a brisk flame. There was no denying the fact. Paradise — uninsured Paradise — was in real danger.

"Water!" he cried. "No, I want a broom!"

"Broom!" said Puelvir scornfully. "What can a man do with a broom?" She meant to give him what she thought best; and she did; for while he was crawling under to beat the fire out with a piece of planking that he found there, Puelvir emptied two pails of hogshead water through the broad cracks of the piazza. This, and Hensleigh's plank, successfully extinguished the blaze. But it also extinguished him.

He crawled out meekly, dripping from head to foot. Corona met him, trembling violently.

"Is it out?" she gasped, "all out?"

"I should think it ought to be."

"Thank God!" interpolated Corona.

"Feel of me!" he answered wetly.

But Puelvir was not satisfied. She had brought two more pailfuls of water, and she now energetically emptied them lengthways over the piazza. This time the flood caught Hensleigh in the ankles as he was coming up the steps.

"Oh, you poor fellow!" cried Corona. "Let me get you some dry things."

This wifely exhibition of tenderness, which he had not at all deserved, or expected, broke down what little obstinacy Puelvir's hydropathic treatment had left in Alexander. Even a bulldog is conquered by a pail of water, and Hensleigh was a gentleman.

"You poor darling!" Forgetting that he was dripping he took his wife in his arms. "I am so sorry! You were perfectly right, and I was entirely wrong. I 'll — I 'll never smoke again " —

"Until the house is insured," interrupted Corona archly.

"Well — ah — yes," admitted Alexander.

"And that will be to-morrow morning."

They laughed and kissed. Her fluffy, light evening dress lay contentedly in his soaked, corduroy embrace.

"This must never happen again," he said after a damp, but happy silence. "Love is too precious, and marriage is too sacred."

"It was dreadful!"

"It was blasphemy!" he cried; "and we 'll promise by this — by this — and this — that it shall never happen again."

"It never shall," said Corona solemnly. But in her heart of hearts she wondered if it ever would.

CHAPTER V

DEEP-SEA FISHING

THE memory of that brief, but what might have proved a serious disagreement, cast a spell of tenderness upon the two married lovers. Each made it a point to yield to the other until the only one in Paradise who had a will of her own was Puelvir.

"Don't you want to take a walk to Grace's Cove?"

"Not unless you want to, dear."

"But I don't care to unless you do."

"It's just as you say."

So like two stupid angels, they would stand and devour each other with tender, happy glances, having brought action to a disinterested deadlock, that seems insupportable to the world which has passed through such married nonsense, and which is an indispensable condition to those just joined in the holy toils of matrimony.

Corona would not eat strawberries unless Alexander picked out the largest ones for himself; and Alexander absolutely refused to select the giant berries unless she promised on her wedding ring to eat them. Ah, if those little idiocies, at which the world guffaws, only because it associates them with the honeymoon, would but last through married life, then we should consider them the expression of the greatest wisdom possible to poor humanity.

They were standing together, Corona leaning on her husband's shoulder, saying good-night, as they always did, to the red flash-light on the Point, the friend that understood them better than any other, when Alexander said, without any apparent effort: —

"I'm going out fishing to-morrow, and expect to start about five. I will slip out without waking anybody up."

In reality, Alexander had dreaded to give this information, very much as a boy is reluctant to explain to his well-armed father obvious discrepancies in his speech and conduct. With the wiliness of a serpent, the bridegroom had chosen this particular time so that in the darkness of the night their mutual emotions might be invisible to each other.

Corona's only answer was to let her arm drop gently from the culprit's shoulder. But to the man, her silence was as eloquent as a bombardment.

"You see," he went on with hollow cheerfulness, "I've engaged Father Morrison, and as soon as the traps are drawn, we are going to start right out with the Flash, so as to be on the grounds" —

"The *Flash!*" interrupted Corona incredulously. "Why, she capsized with Zero and three boys four years ago. Father Morrison himself rowed out and picked them up. Three clung to the bottom and one was caught in the trap. It took two hours to resuscitate him" — Corona stopped only to gain breath. She continued with staccato distinctness. "Then two boarders took the Flash out the next year, and she went over in a squall. The next "— But Hensleigh interrupted.

"Probably they did n't know how to tack, or drop their canvas."

"No," said Corona severely. "The halyards got tangled. The next year the Flash went out with a fishing party, got caught in the fog, and was n't heard of for three days. There were two tugs looking for her all of the time, and one was nearly run down."

"But that was n't the fault of the Flash," observed Alexander desperately.

"No?" questioned Corona with infinite sarcasm. Then she melted. "I — I cannot — I simply cannot stand your going in the Flash. It would be an eternal separation. It is nothing less than suicide." She gave a little gulp, and clung again appealingly to her husband's arm.

"There, there, girl!" — Alexander's tone was as soothing and reassuring as an eiderdown quilt, but his heart was a bit impatient. "You don't mean, dearest," he went on, quietly, "that you don't want me to go fishing at all?"

"N-n-no!" Corona's voice came with a catch and a gasp, as if she had been suddenly struck with spray in the face. "I wouldn't have you give up your trip for anything, especially if you have made an engagement with Father Morrison."

Alexander smiled inaudibly. An irrevocable engagement with the lobster man, as if he were a banking magnate! But this was just like Corona. The poorer and plainer her neighbors were the more she seemed to think of them. Nevertheless, he stood to his purposes, feeling, manlike, that if he gave in an inch now, his future independence wouldn't be worth mentioning; and she, poor woman, felt that if she did not concur in his resolution, happiness might take flight from their cottage window. "Besides," she continued heroically, "a man must have his pleasures, even if they do take him away from his wife; only I beg of you, *don't* go in the Flash."

"Very well, what shall I go in?"

"I should n't object to a tug."

"A tug! Why don't I charter a Cunarder? You must be crazy, child. You never used to be foolish like that. I always thought you were a sensible woman."

"But I was n't married then, dear. It makes all the difference in the world."

"I suppose so. Very well. I will charter a tug to go two miles off the Point fishing. It will probably cost me fifty dollars, — but as long as you will feel that I am safe, I suppose " — he stopped sternly.

But this sarcasm was all lost on Corona. She was literally immolating herself upon the altar of self - sacrifice. What would have been the most natural thing in the world two months ago, now seemed to her wedded apprehension a desperate undertaking. The placid ocean that used to be so sympathetic was now suddenly changed to torpid malignity. For Alexander to go out upon the water without her was like trusting him to a raging, personal enemy. And

now before her imagination, congested by
the fear that feeds on love, there swept picture after picture of horrible Atlantic scenes
— of shipwreck, of hunger and thirst and
exposure, of torturing death, and of the
rescue that came an hour too late. These
tales of Fairharbor woes, that had formerly
glided like distant tragedies from her memory, now stabbed her heart, and caused her
a suffering too real for the man to com-
prehend. Nevertheless, resolutely, with a
devotion that husbands never can understand and less appreciate, she hid her apprehension in her soul, concealed the withering
anxiety that she knew she must bear until
he safely returned, and smilingly said: —

"Forgive me, dear, my anxiety about the
Flash. I take it all back. You are certainly a good enough sailor to be the best
judge. We don't consider the Flash a safe
boat around here. Having said that, it is
all that is necessary. Puelvir will have a
cup of coffee ready for you and put you up
some lunch, and I hope you will have a

splendid day's fishing." No one knows what that speech cost the new wife. Hensleigh may have had an inkling, and a tinge of remorse may have touched him as he accepted her renunciation.

"There!" he said. "That's the kind of a wife I like." And, foolish woman that she was, she deluded herself into thinking that his little appreciation might more than pay her for the torture of letting him have his own way.

But she did not sleep that night. Every hour or so she timidly put out her hand to be sure that her husband was really there. She had a feeling that these might be the last hours on earth together.

The next morning broke with a motionless sea and sky. A gentle haze idealized the harbor and made it look like the image of a dream. Picturesque dories were lazily creeping to their traps at which already a small fleet of shore fishing sloops were slothfully anchored, their sails hanging in listless folds, waiting for the ruffles on the water to chase the calm.

"At any rate," thought Corona, "he can't drown in a calm, or be run over. God is good to me." And her heart rose. Aloud she said: —

"What a glorious day, and how the fish will bite!"

"Yes," said Hensleigh with the good-humored aggressiveness of a man who is in the process of successfully carrying his point, "and you may thank your stars you are not going to broil out there all day in a ground swell with not a breath of air."

"But I was n't invited, anyway," Corona observed demurely as she took the milk pitcher from Puelvir and poured the white cascade into the thick summer goblet.

"Hm-m! I — had n't thought of that; but if you 'd really like to go, you had better — put on " — he flunked helplessly like a schoolboy.

"Never mind me, dear," interrupted Corona with a heroic air, "this is your day, and I hope you will be happier than I. I would n't spoil it by going for the world.

And is n't this better than starting out from an old boarding-house without any one to look after you?"

The look that Alexander gave his wife for answer was interrupted by a hoarse call from the rocks.

"Air ye ready?" bawled Father Morrison. "Them tinkers will all be sold out an' ye 'll hev to bait up with squid if ye don't slip yer moorin' purty quick."

Corona gave her husband's arm the last tender pat while he bent to kiss her. She tried to give the parting a light appearance. But, in truth, she felt as if it were the last. She set her teeth in her tongue to keep from crying. Alexander, obtuse — whether willfully or not, who shall say? — to this feminine suffering, picked up his lunch basket, and ran like a boy down the slippery granite. His heart was full of her tenderness and of the delight of the home which his soul had craved all these years. At the same time, his mind was distracted with the idea of sport. It would be an interesting study to inquire into the number of happy homes that have been blasted by the masculine insanity to go forth and kill. How many athletic men are there who would deny themselves what they call "sport" for the sake of a little wife at home? It may not be impossible that in the next world murdered partridges and deer and salmon and trout may be allowed a game preserve stocked with the men who hunted them; a state of retribution where the open season for this sport extends throughout the whole year, and where pigeons may have shooting-matches to see how many heartless humans they can wing in a hundred shots.

But Hensleigh did not think of these things. He was a little restless under his wife's surveillance.

"You will take good care of him, Father Morrison, for *my* sake?" fluttered plaintively over the water after them as they lustily rowed the Flash to the nearest trap. "As if I were a boy!" he thought to himself, forgetting for the moment what he very well knew, that every wife looks upon her husband as a big boy, a cross between a lover and a baby, and that this is the most natural, maternal, and loveliest thing in the world. And soon he forgot the loneliness which he had left behind, and only thought of keeping cool his glistening bait for which he had paid twenty-five cents a bucket, and of getting upon the ground before the rest of the professional fleet.

.   .   .   .

It was about nine o'clock that morning when Father Morrison cast a look of unutterable disgust into the water. The two men had been fishing doggedly.

"That's the tenth shark I've hooked," he muttered with a salty expletive, "and I'm danged" — Here he took his line by the lead, and swinging it in a three quarters circle, he dexterously brought the head of the white, squirming, vicious little shark down upon the rail of the boat with a thud — "if I'll throw her out again! I don't fish fur dogs fur no man." His voice fell into inarticulate growls as he cut the hook out of the dogfish's mouth. When that was done, he looked up at Hensleigh from under his bushy white eyebrows as if that innocent groom were the cause of this disastrous strike of fish.

But Hensleigh did not say anything. His line dipped. He recovered it with a jerk, and now began to haul up the sixteen fathoms of cod-line hand over hand.

"*That*'s no dog!" he finally exclaimed in exultation, as the struggling line came in harder and harder, and he paused for a moment to rest.

"Keep her taut!" cried Father Morrison, interested for the first time that hot, calm day. He put out his gnarled hand to feel the line.

"Don't touch it! I'll haul her up myself." Alexander spoke impatiently. "Have the gaff ready. There she comes!" Hensleigh bent over to greet his capture, and peered into the ugliest, most horrible face he had ever seen. One look into the coun-

tenance of that fish was enough for the old
man. He dropped the gaff in despair, and
fell back upon the thwarts with a grunt.

"What is it?" asked Alexander helplessly. "How shall I get it off?" He
picked up the gaff and put it teasingly in
the creature's mouth. This the fish bit in
two as if it were a toothpick.

"You'd better cut the line," observed
the old fisherman with dry irritation.
"You'll never get that hook out. It's
worse than a dog."

Hensleigh gave a sickened look at the
monstrous gray distortion, that snapped at
him madly.

"What is it?" he asked, feeling dizzy as
he bent to cut the intruder off.

"What?" repeated Father Morrison sav-
agely, — "what is it? It's a *cat!*"

When Hensleigh had determined upon
this fishing trip, he had made up his mind
to make the most of this his first outing
since his marriage. While he had no idea
of inflicting pain upon the wife whom he

loved with all his heart, his mind, and his soul, nevertheless he had his theories. Most married men have. One of Hensleigh's ran interrogatorily through his mind in some such fashion as this: would not his whole married life be happier if he accustomed her soon to the thought of his absence? It seldom occurs to the man that while he is being diverted by business, travel, or pleasure, the wife whom he leaves behind may prefer the monotonous miseries of waiting and watching, to the forgetfulness which distraction makes possible. He had never understood before marriage that Corona had this insensate fear of the water. Probably she did not know it herself. Therefore, Alexander was really unaware of the extent of the suffering he was inflicting. He was not in a hurry. Not a cod, not a haddock, a hake, or any other respectable fish were on the grounds that morning. The voracious dogfish had driven everything off, and while the professional fishermen, well knowing the futility of earning a living under such conditions, had long since gone home in disgust, the amateur had clung to a vain hope and had stayed on, notwithstanding Father Morrison's grunts and expletives.

"We 've brought our lunch, and we might as well stay," explained Hensleigh apologetically. "The luck will turn with the tide."

"Jess as you say," observed the old fisherman briefly. He was paid by the hour, and could afford to sprawl idly on the thwarts and smoke his pipe. The ability to resign one's self to absolute laziness is as peculiar to fishermen when there 's nothing to catch as it is to a tramp. While Hensleigh was pulling up his malicious catfish, which is the marine devil of the Fairharbor coast, he was thinking how happy his wife was, reading in her favorite hammock, and how proud she would be of him when he came home carrying Atlantic trophies.

In reality, the lady was at that moment on top of the Point lighthouse, peering through a three-foot telescope, catching, as she struggled to understand the mysteries of monocular focus, occasional glimpses of water, and rarer ones of the Flash.   With her naked eyes Corona could distinguish the boat very well as it bobbed up and down at anchor two miles or so away, beyond the red whistling buoy.   This made her very happy.   But her vision, trained by several seasons to cloud effects, noticed something else far off on the southeastern horizon.   It was a dense gray-white cloud bank that seemed to be creeping near and nearer.   Once, as she looked again, she noticed a coaster disappear behind it.   Then she knew it was fog!   Up to this point her miseries had been those of the imagination.   Now they began, indeed, to be real enough.   The lighthouse keeper heard her cry out piteously: —

"This is terrible!   The fog is coming in!   They will be lost!   Why don't they see it?   We must warn them.   Oh, won't you ring the bell?"

"There, there!" said the keeper kindly. "It is coming on thick in course of time. But he'll be all right. Yes, I'll let her off for you."

He gallantly ran down the lighthouse steps in direction of the bell. Now, it was at this very moment that Hensleigh caught the cat. It was the last ounce that turned the scale of his pleasure into nausea.

"This is simply abominable!" he cried out. "There's no fishing, and this ground swell is — er — very un—humph—fortunate. Let's pull up and go home. There! Do you hear that bell? Hark!"

The ancient lobsterman crossed his rubber boots, and looked at Hensleigh with amusement partly veiled by sarcasm.

"You kin pull up," he said shortly between puffs, "an' you kin pull her home. There ain't no air; there'll be one by'n' by from the east'ard. I've worked them sweeps gettin' her here all I'm goin' to. It's about noon, an' I'm goin' to make the coffee." The old man, having delivered himself of this mutinous sentiment, bowed himself into the little cuddy, and pretty soon dense smoke added to the disenchantment which the mention of lunch had inflicted upon Hensleigh's imagination.

Again the fog-bell tolled, this time with greater vigor.

"He's salutin' boarders reckless, that's what he's up to," explained Father Morrison from below.

But Hensleigh lay in the cockpit, his heel upon the wooden seat. He was thinking in a turbulent manner how the swell had increased since he had stopped fishing, and what an idiot he was to go out when the dogfish had "struck." In a reeling sort of a way he casually considered how much better off he would have been if he had stayed at home with Corona.

The Flash rolled, her boom creaked at the mast, her sails flapped, her rope swished, and every time she rose the anchor line came out of the water with a hiss. These noises, so discordant and varied, became monotonous when repeated ten times a minute, and soon they even lulled Hensleigh into a doze, in which the distant bell seemed like a faint clear call. He only turned an ashen face of protest when invited to step below and partake of lunch. So Father Morrison, with a meaning and indulgent smile, ate it all up, and then filled the cuddy with contented smoke, while his passenger lapsed into a fitful and dizzy sleep.

CHAPTER VI

THE POINT

It might have been three o'clock when Father Morrison was aroused from the doze into which he so easily drifted after a good meal and a consolatory pipe. A puff of dampness, that only could have blown straight from the east, impelled the mariner to immediate action. It was a danger signal which even his somnolent senses could not disregard.

His rheumy eyes looked anxiously up at the blue sky that shone down into the narrow cuddy. But when the old man stuck his head out, he uttered a cry of alarm. For, not a hundred yards away, an irresistible bank of fog bore down upon them. Even as it advanced, lightly dancing upon the darkening waters, it thrust out huge, fleecy tentacles, as if it were alive, a devouring kraken of the air.

But Hensleigh opened his eyes with heavy languor. His back was turned to the translucent terror of the sea.

"What's up?" he asked indifferently. At that moment an arm of fog darted ahead, and spread its fingers over the sun, and obscured it as if with a film of milk. Then an icy breath shot forth.

"Ha! what's that?" he cried with dull apprehension.

"Get up there, you landlubber you!" Father Morrison uttered these gruff words with the deadly fear, and with the resentment of a man who has betrayed a sacred trust. He spoke, also, with the license given only to the autocracy of a captain, and only on his own vessel.

"It's fog, I tell you! Haul in on that buoy-line as ye never hauled before! Git that anchor in while I h'ist the throat an' peak! Goramighty! What'll *she* say?"

Hensleigh jumped to his feet. His dizziness had instantly disappeared. He stared at the insistent fog, and then, as if by mutual agreement, the two men looked at each other. Each had but one thought that leaped into instant being. It was not the terror of fog, or of shipwreck, or death. It was the fear of a woman.

It was in vain that they tried to hide this unmanly feeling by a sickly, pretentious smile. In that brief interchange of mute despair, it occurred to both of them that perhaps it might be better if they should never return. Then the fog swept by them in rolling avalanches. The bell rang out in quick, impassioned strokes — in real earnest now. It called — but even as it called, the Flash was cut off from all the world. They were alone upon the deep.

It was pitiful to see how Father Morrison fumbled in putting up the mainsail. His hands trembled and dropped the halyards repeatedly. During all these years "she" had trusted him; he had been an honored guest at her marriage, and now — it seemed as if a blight thicker than the fog itself had darkened his life. He could never look her in the face again. He knew too well where she was. His seafaring ears interpreted the peculiar toll of that bell, — a sound that could never have come from a well-regulated lighthouse keeper whose mind was undisturbed by visitors. A personal alarm, not a general sense of duty, was behind that nervous warning. She was in the lighthouse hours ago. She had seen the mantle that God had laid upon them while he slept at his watch.

But Hensleigh said to himself: "She's safe at home, and has n't noticed this yet. Perhaps we can get in before the fog strikes the shore. If not — whew!" With alternate hopes and tremblings, he pulled in the anchor line hand over hand, oblivious to the red, poisonous filaments of the medusa, that slimed his fingers and stung them. After what seemed to Father Morrison a prehistoric era, the Flash, with boom well to port, was headed homeward as well as Fairharbor skill could steer, to the double call of the whistling buoy and the lighthouse bell, each of which in mournful antiphony seemed to shriek for the dying and to toll for the dead.

"I suppose you 've got a compass aboard," Hensleigh asked, sitting on the other side of the tiller, with his coat buttoned to his chin, and the fog drizzling from his beard.

The ancient mariner shook his head impatiently.

"Do you mean to say that you have come out here without a compass? How do you expect to get her in?" For the first time a fear other than that of woman invaded the passenger's breast.

"Look here, young man," the skipper turned upon him a white, shaggy brow, under which his bleared eyes burned with rare energy, "a little easterly like this don't make no difference to me. I 've run her in a thousand times in wuss than this, an' if ye 'll let me alone, I 'll bring ye in to *her* ez safe ez a lobster in a pot. I kinder reckon we 'd better stick together in this little muss, an' say ez little about it ez pos-

sible. I hain't needed a compass fur forty
year, an' I don't propose to begin now."

For answer Alexander laid his hand upon
the scaly fist that grasped the tiller. Then
he said softly: —

"I don't care for myself, but" —

"Hullo! What 's that? Ship ahoy,
there! Sheer off, will yer? Put your hellum hard up!" bawled the old man, standing up in his excitement. With one turn
of the tiller he had brought the little Flash
up into the wind. There was a bubbling as
of many brooks. There was a swishing as
of a thousand churns. A huge, threatening
beak poised over them for a moment. Then
a cloud of canvas sped from under the
cloud of fog. The long bay of the fog-horn,
the seaman's drone of warning, grated upon
the damp air. The Flash, drifting helplessly
to windward, bumped the gurried side of
the scudding fisherman. If it had been on
the other side, the long booms would have
dismasted the little boat, and perhaps
drowned its occupants.

A crowd of men looked curiously over the rail down at the two.

"Hullo," shouted one, "old Daddy Morrison! Ye'd better run in, old man, where ye belong — you're lost, out here!"

There was a rude chorus of laughter, a gurgling such as only a sucking rudder can make, and the insolent ghost had been swallowed up.

"That was a mighty narrow shave!" said Hensleigh, when his heart had stopped beating enough for him to talk.

But the old skipper, who had made up his mind what course to pursue as soon as the danger was really over, answered as nonchalantly as possible, albeit with a foreign tremor in his husky voice: —

"Oh, no! That warn't nothing. That happens every day. You'll get used to it when you've fished as much as me."

Hensleigh, who did not suspect that Father Morrison had all the burden he could bear, and was making the last magnificent bluff of his life, answered tartly: —

"That may be. You may like that sort of a thing, but I don't. Get out the horn, and I'll blow it while you steer. We ought to have had it out before."

Then up spoke Father Morrison, and in a petulant tone he uttered these memorable words: —

"There ain't no horn aboard." Not daring to look at his passenger, the old man stroked his white beard, stained red under the mouth, and peered vaguely into the wall of fog.

"*No fog-horn!*" repeated Hensleigh incredulously. " Do you mean that you have gone out on this rickety boat with neither compass nor fog-horn? *What will Mrs. Hensleigh say?*" This last question was asked in a menacing stage whisper.

"If she knows on it," — Father Morrison spoke with the deliberation, with the threatening nodding of the head, and with the gruff accent of one who takes his last stand for life, — "if she ever finds it out, there ain't no more lobsters fur her, nor sails fur you. Our famblies will be strangers."

"If you can assure her that there is absolutely no danger in a little fog like this,
and forget to mention little incidents like
those of the dogfishes and the cat — I will
undertake to preserve your reputation for
seamanship intact with my wife." As Hensleigh spoke, twinges of remorse tweaked his
heart. To withhold information is sometimes the greater sin. He looked at the old
man with renewed interest. They had become partners in dissimulation. He felt as
if they ought to be arrested for conspiracy.

"Done!" said Father Morrison with a
slight twinkle in his faded eyes; and with
that, the two clasped guilty hands. "Now,"
said the skipper in a matter-of-fact tone,
and with a face that was cleared with relief,
"I have shaped her course more easterly
towards the shore so as to keep her out of
the channels, and if you'll take the hellum,
I'll go for'ard and sense for the rocks.
You need n't be afeard; you steer her ez I
say."

Alexander Hensleigh now took the tiller

with a feeling of profound responsibility. Neither of the two men felt inclined to talk any more. They had now approached quite near to the Point — the tongue of land that ended in the white government station and the fog-bell, which tolled its warning in precise intervals. Here and there in the water were the black buoys of sunken lobster pots, and, seeing these, Father Morrison felt entirely at home. As he had explained, a fog meant absolutely nothing to him. The more dense, the more he pitted his forty years of harbor and coast experience against it. It was not the 'fog he feared, — it was the lady.

"Ease her off a little! Hard up! Give her another p'int to the south'ard!" He gave these and similar orders in a low, penetrating voice, and these the landsman executed with zeal and sense.

All at once a rasping, disagreeable, high-pitched, squeaky bark rose above the rumble of the breakers not many fathoms away.

"It's Matthew Launcelot!" cried Hensleigh, starting up. "It's the dog! Mrs. Hensleigh's on the Point waiting for me. What shall I do?" His own anxiety for her now reciprocated the misery which he knew that she suffered on his account. He also felt like a boy caught playing hookey. The terrier, as if scenting the approach of his not too well-beloved master, yapped viciously and shrilly.

The fog-bell replied with a solemn Boom — Boom! Still, the shore was not in sight, although the Flash was scudding along only a few yards away, ready to round the Point, and tack for home.

"Keep still, Matthew!" The clear voice of a woman dominated the surf. This was more than Hensleigh could bear. He stood up in the stern, looking almost as tall as the mast in the magnifying mist.

"Corona! Hullo! Corona, dear! I'm all right. I'm" —

"*Alec!*" came the harrowing call from the other side of the opaque barrier. "Is that you?"

"Yes, my dear!"

"Oh, how *could* you? Where *are* you?
Come right ashore where you are! The
Lady is here to take you home. We 've
waited here all day, and not a soul of us
has had a mouthful of dinner!"

It must be confessed that Alexander was
much moved by this address. He was just
about to advise his wife to get into the
buggy and drive home and meet him at the
wharf, when Father Morrison cried out suddenly: —

"Hard up there! Keep off! keep off, I
say!"

Matthew Launcelot, having recognized
Hensleigh's voice, was barking with the reluctant welcome which he reserved for his
new master. He interrupted everything
that was said, and did not assist that poise
of thought which the situation required.

In his excitement, the landlubber did just
the opposite from what he had been ordered.
He put the tiller hard down, and the little
boat, scudding before the increasing wind,

careened shoreward like a swooping gull.
Then the fog opened, so close were they to
land.   It disclosed Corona standing above
them on a jut of granite, while beneath her
the smooth rollers broke into white foam,
and chased each other up and down a broad
green fissure.

"Oh, Alec!" she cried in ignorant rap-
ture as the Flash appeared suddenly to her
view, "I'm so glad you're safe! Dinner
will be entirely spoiled." She did not notice that the mainsail flapped uselessly, and
that the wind and breakers were carrying
the boat irresistibly upon the rocks.

But Father Morrison uttered a terrible
oath. With the agility of a boy he darted
aft to the helm. Hensleigh, paralyzed by the
disaster which his unpardonable careless-
ness had brought upon them, with instinct
to be as near to his wife as possible, dropped
the tiller, passed the old skipper with equal
rapidity, and stood at the bow, with one
arm about the swaying mast. His attitude
was clearly one of heroism, and was a faint

reminder of Casabianca of burning noto-
riety. But Hensleigh's state of mind was
one of biting humiliation. To have caught
no fish was maddening enough, but to end
the day by running ashore in a fog, and
being drowned at his wife's feet —

The ill-fated Flash was lurched nearer to
the reef. In a few seconds it would all be
over. No one could cling in this rolling,
easterly swell to the rocks, made more slippery than a perpendicular ice pond by the
undertow upon the heartless seaweed. Agonized, he looked up at his wife. And she
looked down upon him with a white, set
fright upon her beautiful face, as she suddenly realized her husband's fatal danger.
Thus, with eyes cemented together in that
brief moment which preceded the catastrophe, and which is always more horrible than
the fulfillment itself, the two awaited the
end.

There was a rising upon the third crest.
There was a series of fateful bumps. There
was a crunching and a grinding, a lurching

and a groaning, as if the poor old Flash protested from her very ribs against this untoward end. This was followed by a cascade of foam that covered the vessel, and a final thrust as if the great Atlantic had given the fishing-boat a playful dig with its little finger. Still, Hensleigh grasped the mast in the rigid embrace of despair. He meant to go down with his colors flying. He did not notice that the Flash had resumed its even keel, and had not begun to be dashed to kindling wood. But he was aroused from his premortuary reverie by a coarse command: —

"Hello there, you blanked idgit! Why don't ye step ashore there lively, before the next comber wets yer pants!"

Hensleigh's eyes, which had become almost glazed, now opened as with a galvanic shock. To his surprise, he noticed that dry land extended itself indefinitely before him. Above him stood his wife. He could almost touch her. In fact, she bent over and reached down her arm. He clasped her

firm hand, and stepping from the rail of
the Flash, he put his left foot in a little
crack in the rocks, unwet by the risen tide,
and in a second he had his wife in his arms.
The infinite separation, the awful fog, the
terrible danger, the providential escape —
even Father Morrison — all, all were forgotten in that rapturous embrace. The lighthouse keeper turned his head delicately
away, and tried to repress a rising sob.
He was used to great dramas, but not to
great love.

At last the lovers, satisfied that they still
had each other, unclasped and looked about.
It suddenly occurred to them that Father
Morrison might have offered up his life to
save his passenger. They looked down for
the martyr. There stood their trusty friend
leisurely lowering the mainsail, and the
waters lapped at him in vain. He caught
their anxious glance, and answered it quizzically.

"Ye need n't be skeered. Ye see, this is
the only landin'-place on the hull coast, and

puffektly safe at high tide. Ye said ye
wanted him right now, an' when a woman
gets sot, an' makes a p'int on 't, there ain't
nothing else to do, so I steered her right in.
That 's all."

He bent to tie his frayed rope stops about
the worn mainsail with the same peaceful
air that he would have exhibited at his own
mooring.

"But was n't it awfully dangerous?"
asked Corona solemnly.

By this time Matthew Launcelot had
come to himself. He had leaped upon the
deck, and was squealing at Father Morrison's legs to be caressed.

"Dangerous!" shouted the old man contemptuously, as he put the little dog into
a fold of the sail and stroked its bony head.
"I don't suppose ye mean to insult me,
Miss Corona, but I gen'rally land here
twic't a season an' sometimes more. There
ain't a safer nor a cosier berth on the coast,
specially when ye want to make the lighthouse or the P'int."

The keeper bit his lips. Father Morrison calmly took down the jib. His face did not relax its serenity. Corona scanned it closely, and then breathed a sigh of relief. She had always trusted Father Morrison. Why should she not now, especially as he had brought her husband to her so safely, so promptly, and with such wonderful skill? Truly, he was the best skipper on the whole coast.

Alexander opened his mouth generously to explain his careless part of · the performance, but out of the tail of the lobsterman's windward eye he observed a warning gleam. He only said, thinking he might as well keep up his own reputation, —

"Shall I put the fish in the buggy, Coro?" But Corona had turned away.

"I 'm — pretty tired," she said weakly. "Let us get right home. And, Alec, you must thank the keeper. He has been very patient with me to-day. As for a fish, I never want to see one again!"

When the couple had crossed the creek,

and the buggy was well out of sight, the two men who were left gave each other a look which it would take a library to interpret.

"Say, uncle," observed the lighthouse keeper slowly. "How in —— did you do it? I thought you were gone, sure. And so natural-like!"

"Never you mind. It's did, and he's safe, thank God! I'll come down to-night when the tide serves, an' I guess we kin shove her off, an' if not — I'll only charge him fifty dollars. He'll see the p'int. But *she* won't never know."

"Not if I can help it. It's between us, uncle." Then, with great wonder at the miraculous deliverance of boat and crew, the light-keeper, learned above most men of the coast in the dangers of the sea, said gently: "Gor! I would n't hurt her fur the world. She's a lady, she is."

And over the rugged face of the old fisherman there stole a look of tenderness and of solemn gratitude. This glorified him into a different man.

CHAPTER VII

THE MARCH OF PROGRESS

"WHY, there's the Bobby T.!" exclaimed Corona. She put a pound or two more pull into her left arm, and the Sandpiper turned its blunt prow towards a half-hidden cove. The Sandpiper was Corona's rowboat; a dingey, the fishermen called it; it was a cross between a dory and a skiff.

The two had now formed the habit of rowing after supper. Corona liked to do all the nautical work. She brought the boat in hand over hand on the hauling-line which was fastened to two broken oar handles driven into a cleft of the red granite. She deftly untied the wet sailor's hitch while Alexander, carrying the straight-bladed oars, admiringly looked on. Hensleigh had no objection to being rowed out into the pathway of the setting sun, and back into the red avenue of the rising moon. They filled these happy hours with lovers' "little language." When Corona rested on her oars and sang softly, Hensleigh beat a tinkling time with his palm upon the resonant sea. Sometimes he rocked the boat, and the hollow "chunk!" of the flat bow sounded in the stillness like a tertiary frog. Now they drifted with the tide up the harbor, and now the silent current carried them out into the breadth of the bay. One evening they studied the marvelous color transformations, cheek to cheek, so that neither should miss the slightest miracle that the other saw, and their hearts were full of awe, and their tongues of silence, because they were permitted to live together in such a world. "Dear," Corona would whisper, fearing to mar by a breath the transcendent loveliness, "Heaven cannot be more beautiful;" and he answered with a solemn inclination. Indeed, there are no more wonderful sunsets in all the world than those at Fairharbor, and the tints that are the despair of artists are often the inspiration of lovers.

This evening they started home when the dew was heavy, and the thwarts and the gunwales were wet beneath their hands. Hensleigh looked up at his wife's exclamation, and in the dimness of the twilight saw two unfamiliar masts in a familiar place.

" What on earth is the Betsy T.? " he asked lazily.

"The *Bobby* T. It 's our landlord's fishing-boat. He 's been off more than six weeks on a trip to Block Island, so Zero says, and they were beginning to be very anxious about him. I am glad he 's come home."

Hensleigh showed no enthusiasm on the subject. It seemed as remote to him as that other which Corona introduced a few minutes ago. What had he to do with Heaven or with landlords? Honeymoon and Paradise were enough for him. They swept by the little fishing-schooner, bumped up against the weeds, hauled the Sandpiper out, and crept up the damp rocks hand in hand. Puelvir met them on the piazza.

"Ye never can tell what mought not happen, when ye 'r' out, Miss Corona," she began sepulchrally. "I never did favor that man, and now I know why."

"What man?" asked Corona pleasantly. "The raspberry man?"

"It 's wuss than that. *He* would n't 'a' had the gall. It 's that there landlord of ourn. I wish they 'd put him into a lobster-pot and made bait of him. He 's rose!"

"Rose?" Hensleigh looked around anxiously, expecting to see a man towering from the rocks.

"What *can* have happened?" asked Corona, troubled. She held out her hand for the note, which Alexander deftly took and read aloud by the parlor lamp.

To Miss Corona and Gentleman :

For season of 18—. To rent of 50 sq. ft. ground lease			
To cottage for one tenant	.	.	. $25.00
" two tenants	.	.	. 50.00
Received cash	. .	.	. 25.00
Owe .	. .	.	. 25.00

Received payment,

"Why, I've paid my summer rent! I pay it every spring before I come down," began Corona excitedly. "I hold his receipt. Don't you remember, dear? I paid it *that* day."

"He said," interrupted Puelvir, "that he wa'n't consulted about her marriage. That wa'n't in the contract. He says he's upsot comin' back from Block Island and findin' an extra one on his premises. 'T wa'n't in the bargain, and he's goin' to be paid fur it."

"Great Cæsar's ghost!" ejaculated Hensleigh.

"Dear me, Puelvir!" echoed Corona. It was the only oath she knew, and the maid was used to it.

Puelvir now looked from one to the other with an air of unprecedented embarrassment.

"I'd rather tell ye the rest alone, Miss Corona — worse take him!" she said, doubling up her fists.

Alexander, feeling that he was *de trop*, put his hands in his pockets and walked out on the piazza, whistling. Puelvir's voice now sank to a gruesome whisper, and she looked over her shoulder to be sure that no one was eavesdropping.

"He says, Miss Corona, that if ye should ever have a fambly, he intends to charge twenty-five dollars a head fur each one on 'em. He seems he can't be reconciled to yer gettin' married nohow; and if ye 'd consulted him, and not sprung it on him, he 'd 'a' told ye so. Most of the folks on the P'int feel the same way," added Puelvir with a touch of pardonable malice.

"Dear me, Puelvir!" repeated Corona more faintly than before. "Why, this is terrible!"

"Ye see," added Puelvir in an instructive tone, "every one of 'em around here thinks they own you."

"Give me that bill," said Hensleigh, coming in. "I 'll attend to it. Twenty-five dollars extra is a small matter for the tenancy of Paradise. I 'll go over and see him at once."

Alexander kissed a tear away from the eyes of his troubled wife, put on his hat, and hurried out. Corona expected him to stay a long while, but in about ten minutes he came back. He did not smile. At the sight of his grave face her heart dropped heavily.

"It's no use, dear," began Hensleigh soberly, "to try to bargain with him. I offered to buy the lot we lease. What do you suppose he asked for these fifty square feet?"

"Five hundred dollars?" Corona's eyes brightened.

"Twenty thousand! He said he's going to put up two hotels and run out a steamboat wharf. He spoke about a skating-rink, and mentioned a steam laundry. He threw in a bowling-alley, by the way. He says that fish is played out; that four men of them on the Bobby T. only got two half barrels in six weeks. He's going to sell his boat and live upon his property. He says he's going to haul his land into the march of progress!"

"I came here to have a quiet, peaceful home," said Corona after a long silence. "I built it, I lived in it, and I loved it — I can't stand seeing it spoiled forever — and oh! I *cannot* give it up." Her lip quivered.

"Don't!" he tried to comfort her. "We can easily sell it; in fact, I had an offer for it this evening. He said he 'd swap."

"How much?" scornfully.

"Why, he said he 'd swap the Bobby T. for it."

"The Bobby T. for Paradise? I would n't let him have it for forty thousand dollars!" flashed the outraged householder. "But what shall we do?"

Hensleigh's heart echoed the words, but he had no solution to offer.

For a few days the husband and wife tried to forget the matter, and go on as if nothing had happened. But Alexander came in one morning suddenly, and found his wife with a quivering chin looking out of the northern window. Their landlord and a strange man with a fifty-foot tape were measuring ground. The husband perceived that he must take matters into his own hands, but, as often happened, he missed the opportunity.

"Who is that man?" asked Corona fiercely.

"He is the contractor for the skating-rink, and he's adding a proposition for a band-stand at a very low figure."

"Will you please tell Zero to harness up The Lady?" said Corona decidedly.

"Certainly. But what for?"

"I am going out to hunt up a new home."

"And if you have no objections," Hensleigh smiled dryly, "I should like to go too."

Corona asked Puelvir to put up a lunch, and a supper, too. She added, in a dejected tone, that she didn't know but they'd better lay in stores for a week.

"I shall hunt till I find another Paradise," she firmly announced. But her heart

echoed her own words with a sharp interro-
gation.   Could it be — is it ever permitted
to any soul to possess Paradise more than
once in a lifetime?

Zero brought The Lady.   "We are not
coming back till night," Corona explained.

"Tight?" echoed Zero.   "Yes, the harness is all tight."

"Night," repeated Hensleigh in a comfortable tone.

"All right," replied the boy with a
smile.

"He always hears *me*," observed Alexander with superiority.

Matthew Launcelot, between whom and
The Lady of Shalott existed an irreconcil-
able feud, trotted after the buggy as far as
the gate, and sadly watched it wind up the
little hill.   He did not offer to follow.

Now began a systematic search that lasted
for three days.   They scoured the town and
country.   They inspected the cliffs and
beaches.   They priced shore lots and back
lots, and were asked the same figure for

both. Hensleigh was looking for a house with a lot; Corona for a lot without a house. The man, who had once been worsted in a contest with a builder, said he'd rather camp out than build. But Corona said she'd just as soon sign a contract with Mr. Timbers as with any other archangel. He wouldn't cheat her for the price of a whole trip of halibut. Not having a Fairharbor education, Alexander's mind received no idea from this ten-thousand-dollar figure.

The location of Paradise was conceded to be the most beautiful on the Massachusetts coast. To give this up seemed to Corona like sacrificing a high ideal to a penny fact.

"How can I do it?" she exclaimed passionately.

Twenty-six views, including sixteen houses — cottages and Queen Annes, villas and bungalows — fluoresced before their weary gaze. Their eyes had become Roentgen rays after these few days' experience. When they examined the outside of a house they found it unnecessary for them to go within.

They spent the first day riding around the Cape; the second day in driving down the coast, and the third day, in despair, they went to Carriesquall. Alexander drove. He had never been in Carriesquall, and was touched by this beautiful Indian name. Corona looked about retrospectively, but The Lady of Shalott began to act very strangely. Her head went down and her heels went up. Her mane and tail blew wildly in the wind.

"She's running away!" said Corona.

"Running away!" exclaimed Alexander contemptuously, sawing on her bits with all his might. He was a man of a good deal of muscle, and to have a horse get the best of him in the presence of his new wife was exasperating.

"I beg pardon," Corona gently remarked. "She does look as if she were walking to a funeral. Whoa!"

"I'll do my own whoaing!" Hensleigh

shouted, now rising to his feet and twisting the reins about his hands. "That's no way tó talk to a horse, anyway. Shh! Back! Whoa there! *Whoa!*"

By this time the horse had taken the bit between her teeth, and was bolting down the street at a mad pace. There were no citizens in sight. Only a few women looked out of the windows calmly. The street seemed to end in Ipswich Bay. The horse had every appearance of intending to sunder the tie between herself and her passengers in the water. Alexander became very pale. The situation ceased to be a talking matter. All at once the buggy gave a tremendous lurch, turned a sudden corner on two wheels, and The Lady made straight for a barn door. Unhappily, this was only half open. The horse got in, but the buggy couldn't. The terrified passengers tumbled out. Then The Lady turned her beautiful head around, regarded her owner with a pleased expression, and whinnied gently.

At that moment a kindly looking elderly man ran out of the kitchen door.

"Why, this is Northeast Carriesquall!" exclaimed Corona. "I might have remembered. This must be The Lady's old home. Why, you clever horse!" She went up and patted the quivering animal. "How do you do, Mr. Thumb? This is my husband. Alec, this is Mr. Thumb, who sold me an honest horse."

"I should think he did!" growled Hensleigh. "It's the first horse that ever got the best of me."

Mr. Thumb smiled benevolently. "She's some sperited," he admitted; "but my little boy used to ride her bareback. I'm glad to see ye. What can I do for ye?"

"Why, Mr. Thumb, I never saw this place before!" Corona looked out over the sea. There the lonely lighthouse rose like a great white candle from the rocky coast; and on the left the high dunes flanking the beach drifted gradually to a lower level, until the sandy shore melted into the bay far down the desolate arc.

"Why, what a peaceful, pretty place!

You would n't sell it, would you?" asked Corona.

Mr. Thumb, agitated by this stupendous proposition, disappeared in the house to consult his wife. When had anybody in East Carriesquall ever had an offer for a house before? But Hensleigh backed the horse out and suggested that they would ride over the field and see the place. "It is really possible," he admitted.

"The Lady will be quite at home," added Corona pleasantly.

A little cart-path wound through the fields. The two followed it. A luscious strawberry bed was on either side of the road, and The Lady sampled the berries, as she went along, with the air of a horse who had done it before. They had not proceeded a hundred feet when they heard startling cries from behind them.

"Whoa there! Back here! Get out! *Turn around!* Look where ye 're goin'!" shouted Mr. Thumb. He ran after them, gesticulating and vociferating wildly.

"The man must be crazy," said Alexander, driving on. "I'll be hanged if I'll hold up for him!"

At this moment Mr. Thumb's clumsy figure overtook the slowly moving buggy, and he yanked The Lady by the bit.

"Why did n't ye stop when I told ye?" Mr. Thumb's face was pale with terror, and his hands shook with holy rage. "Look ahead there! Can't ye see?"

"I don't see anything," said Hensleigh obstinately. But Corona looked, and she saw hanging from a limb of a tree — on a bough that their buggy must have touched — a black, swaying, living cloud.

"It's *bees!*" cried Mr. Thumb. "Bees a-swarmin'! If ye 'd gone ten feet further I would n't hev answered for yer lives for five minutes. That there mare would 'a' taken ye off the rocks into the Atlantic Ocean! Easy there — easy!"

Stepping softly so as not to awaken the wrath that may easily be fatal to those who intrude upon swarming bees, Mr. Thumb turned the horse in as short an arc as possible. But it was almost too late. A few winged sentinels had discovered the offenders and began to drive them off. They settled upon The Lady. The horse gave a plunge, and before Hensleigh could realize what had happened the two were tearing out of town at the same gait as that by which they had entered. The bees pursued their enemy for two or three miles. Not until the last one flew into the buggy and was "squashed" by Alexander on his own cheek, could he get the horse under control.

"I should think this ended Northeast Carriesquall," he observed when he had at last yanked The Lady to her haunches.

"I should think it ended the whole thing," returned Corona wearily. She was very tired. "I don't know but we can get along where we are," she pleaded. But Alexander looked at her keenly, and with masculine persistence saved her from herself.

"*I* don't mind the racket," he said grimly. "I can stand a laundry blowing off steam every five minutes. A brass band and a season of Fairharbor hops are nothing to me. I rather like a bowling-alley. Two summer hotels, say five hundred guests apiece, turned loose on our rocks and playing banjos on our piazza, only make company for me. I think you're right. I think we'd better stay. A steamboat wharf"—

"Not for a hundred worlds!" she interrupted hotly. "Paradise is lost."

"The serpent has spotted it," suggested her husband.

"Your language is not exactly Scriptural, my dear," replied Corona, trying to smile, "but your facts are correct. There is nothing to be done. We must flee from the wrath to come." When Corona really made up her mind she stuck to it like a limpet on a rock.

Alexander thoughtfully lighted a cigar. They had come back through the town.

They had crossed the Cut Bridge to the westward. They had left the large ice-houses behind and were approaching West Fairharbor and its beautiful estuaries. The Lady of Shalott was trotting lazily. Suddenly they came out of the woods upon the little station. It was deserted. The baggage truck and two side - tracked freight cars gave the place the air of an approaching boom that might become metropolitan. These suggested the hurry and business that were not, but might be. They were the pathetic *amœbœ* of civilization. Bar Harbor was started on less than that.

But Corona was tired out. The pine grove between the station and the river looked attractive. Alexander took the bridle off The Lady and gave her the last of the oats for her supper. Corona had disappeared. Memories of the honeymoon trip flooded her heart like happy music and soothed her perplexed mind. She followed the narrow pine-needle path along which Matthew Launcelot had led them (it seemed to her many months ago) to the hospitable dory. It was about the same hour, and like that other wonderful evening the air was calm and the tide lapped high.

"There ought to be a view here somewhere," she thought. "It must be ideal." She could never see through other people's eyes the scene of their voyage into a united life. Everything about it was glorified. To the left, above her, was a rocky slope. She ran up eagerly. It was not more than a hundred feet or so high. Half way up she turned. Her husband had gone down to the water, and was looking for her vainly.

"Whew—oo!" she tried to whistle. "I 'll race you up the rest of the way!" It was not a fair start, and he knew it; but love gave his feet wings, and she had but reached the summit when he caught his Atalanta in his arms.

"Hush!" she whispered. "Look!"

They looked, and saw to the right Fairharbor Bay, and beyond, the sea. In the

calm a fishing-schooner was being strenu-
ously towed to anchorage by six dories in
line ahead. The little city, with its many
quaint towers that had almost a Moorish
appearance, gave back the changing colors
of the sunset. To the left lay the purple
of Ipswich Bay, and against its darkening
bosom white rolling sand dunes gleamed.
The river crept into a thousand inlets with
oily lassitude, and showed delightful possi-
bilities for the Sandpiper.

"Why, I don't know but I might live
here." Corona thought she had conceded
a great deal. "It is rather pretty."

"Why, child! it's superb!" cried Alexander, taking off his hat. "Here's the
station not three minutes away — the water
right at your feet — a pine grove that is
worth a thousand dollars — the finest kind
of a view, and Ipswich Bay thrown in.
I'll wager I'll get it for fifty dollars an
acre."

They stood for a moment hand in hand.
Not a sound could be heard but the lisping

of the water. It seemed as if they stood alone in all the world. A possible peace crept like a dear friend toward them.

"Well" — said Corona slowly, with a long sigh of surrender.

"I 'll buy it," said Alexander in a business-like way. "Let 's eat our supper."

.   .   .   .

It was nine o'clock and dark when they slowly drove up to the clothes-post in the back yard of Paradise. Corona had not spoken for some time. Matthew Launce-lot and Puelvir and Zero ran out to meet her, all talking and barking together. The light looked out lovingly from the windows, and the soft waves called from the feet of the rocks.

"My dear old home!" said Corona. "How can I — *can* I leave it?"

Her husband put out his hand in the dark buggy to caress her cheek; he found it wet.

.   .   .   .

About two o'clock next morning Alexander woke his wife. "I've got it!" he exclaimed. "I can't keep it to myself. You sha'n't leave Paradise. *We'll move the house!*"

CHAPTER VIII

PARADISE AFLOAT

It was a moving subject, and the family concentrated their attention upon it. After breakfast the next morning Mr. Hensleigh mysteriously disappeared. He came back at twelve o'clock with Mr. Timbers and a strange man. The whole family ran out to meet them. Matthew Launcelot made straight for the stranger's shins.

"I've bought the lot," began Hensleigh joyously, "five acres, water front and the pine grove. It's a splendid lot."

"Hot?" drawled Zero. "Yes, sir, it is hot."

"Aren't you afraid you are going too fast?" Corona asked lovingly but cautiously.

"Dash that dog! Take him off!" exclaimed the strange man.

"Drop him, Matthew!" threatened Alexander. "Let him alone, sir. He's the new house-mover."

Like all pet dogs Matthew understood everything that was said to him in the vernacular. Comprehending the whole situation, he retreated in a dignified way to his mistress' lap, loftily ignoring his mistake.

"This is the house," began Hensleigh with a business-like wave of the hand. "The lot, as I explained, is on that little knoll by the West Fairharbor station. What will you move it there for? I should think it was about — eh — three miles, possibly a little more."

"Hmgh!" snorted the mover. "It's nigh seven. What do you say, George?"

Mr. Timbers, being appealed to, took out his two-foot rule, and, after a few cabalistic measurements in the air, announced that he calculated it was about six miles and seven-eighths. The two mechanics began to examine the house with expert expressions.

After some consultation they both came back shaking their heads.

"'T ain't none of my business," said Mr. Timbers, stroking his chin with a fatherly air, "though I always have looked after this lady till now — you see, I built this house — I should advise ye to stay where ye are."

"We can't," interrupted Puelvir. "He's rose!"

"Circumstances make it undesirable," observed Hensleigh with some dignity. "We have decided to move."

"It's cheaper to sell her," said the mover. "I can't get her over there fur less than seven hundred and fifty dollars, and me out of pocket at that."

"And I couldn't think of doing the carpenter-work on her for less than two hundred and fifty, and I'd be losin' money on it at that price!" added the builder.

"Why, Mr. Timbers," said Corona severely, "you built me the whole house for five." It dawned upon this young matron that her old Fairharbor friends were working her new husband as an unfathomable mine.

"Of course," observed Hensleigh with a smile, "I know that both of you gentlemen would only undertake this as a missionary job. That goes without saying." He gently motioned his wife away. After a few minutes' talk with the two men he returned to Corona. "We've struck a bargain," he said. "The mover will get his permit from the city, and I'll run over and get mine from the landlord." Alexander and the men walked off. The remainder of the family collected and breathlessly discussed the stupendous situation.

"Move the house!" exclaimed Puelvir. "You got to move mine too. My kitchen and bedroom have got to go along."

"Yours shall certainly go," Corona comforted her. But in point of fact, she felt dizzy with the rapidity of this masculine energy that was sweeping through her life. Left to herself she would have been all summer coming to the point. Now it was

done in four days, and even Tom had not
been consulted. The happy wife sighed.
Was she able to stand the pace or not?

"I can't get to and fro nights and mornin's," suggested Zero miserably. There
were real tears in the boy's eyes. "I hope
it 'll get stuck by the Baptist meetin'-
house."

"I bet it will!" cried Puelvir, flopping
her apron wildly around her head. "And
I 'd like to see 'em squoze along through by
where them fish flakes is, alongside of the
mast yard! That 's an uncommon narrer
strip."

"It *is* a little narrow by the post-office,"
added Corona anxiously.

"I know a house got stuck six weeks in
front of the engine-house. There was two
fires happened, and the insurance companies
made the owner pay damages." This was
the longest sentence that Zero had ever
uttered since he had been in Corona's em-
ploy. It must be admitted that she hoped
he would not blossom out into an orator.

But for the second time Hensleigh returned from his landlord sooner than he was expected. On this occasion he walked along with bowed head, and the two men slunk behind him as if they were in disgrace. Corona's agitated heart thumped wildly.

"Well," she said, "tell me the worst first."

"We can't do it; he won't let us move the house across his land."

"Why, he's got to! You must make him, Alec!"

"I can't. It isn't in the lease. You forgot to put it in. There isn't a word about moving."

"But what's the trouble? Why does he object?"

"Corn and cabbages. He says half of his crop would be ruined." Alexander sat down on the piazza chair heavily. "I've offered to pay for the vegetables twice over, but he said it wasn't the money he set by; it was the cabbages, and the hoeing of them."

For the first time Hensleigh's business experience failed him; he saw no way out of the new difficulty. The two mechanics followed his example and dropped upon the steps. They gloomily looked out upon the harbor.

"You can move a house 'most any size, 'most any shape, 'most anywheres, but ye can't move him. Nobody ever could." The house - mover spoke like a graphophone, without expression. But Puelvir, who was calming the agitated group with lemonade, pungently remarked: —

"If it was me I would n't let him get the best of ye. You give me my house and I 'll get it over. I 'll sail it acrost in the Sandpiper. Mebbe he 's sot, but I 'd be sotter!"

"Hm! Hm!" said Mr. Timbers, "that 's an idee! What do you say, Bill?"

The house-mover did not say anything for ten minutes. He finished his lemonade at one gulp, put down his glass, and walked down to the water's edge. His practiced

eye measured the rocks and the coast.
When he returned he uttered these epoch-
making words: —

"If we could hire them two scows layin'
up in the inner cove at a reasonable figger,
and the sea wa'n't too high, and it did n't
blow up a breeze o' wind, and 't wa'n't
thick, and the tide served, I guess I could
jack her up, and skid her out, and tow her
over. I 've tackled wuss jobs than this,
and lost no appetite over 'em yet. What
do you say, George?"

"I hain't seen it done," said Mr. Timbers unenthusiastically, "but if you say
'go,' Bill, there ain't a man on the coast
can beat ye when ye once get at it."

A brief illumination passed over the
house-mover's face at his friend's compli-
ment. He gave his hand a deprecating
jerk. He followed this up with a searching look at Hensleigh, as if to gauge his
daring and originality.

"Do you want us to try it?" he asked.
"If ye do, we 'd better begin to shove her

out as soon as possible. It's a calm spell
now. Ye never can tell what might happen
a little later. Ye couldn't do it in the fall
nohow."

"Dear me!" said Corona, "have we got
to move now? Why, our honeymoon isn't
over yet," she added in a low voice to her
husband. Alexander answered her whisper
with a fond look.

"Just as you .say, dear. But if we've
got to do it the sooner it's over the better."

"Well, I'll run over and measure them
scows and see what the cap'n of the dredger
says. If we can put her through you won't
be out of pocket half what you would if
ye sasshayed her round by the road," remarked the house-mover, discreetly retreating from this domestic episode.

While the two men were gone, Corona
disappeared inside of the house. She went
alone. She went from room to room and
looked out of each window, as if to engrave
its individual view upon her heart forever.
Eve, in that other Paradise, could have

hardly felt sadder when the angel drove her out with the two-edged sword. But Corona had locked her soul. She choked down her feelings, and after a few gulps, and after massaging her cheeks with her handkerchief, she came out to her husband.

"Alec, dear," she began quietly, "I think you are right, and the sooner it goes the better."

Once in a while a man accidentally happens on an intuition, and this time Hensleigh divined the great struggle that made his wife's decision a possibility.

The two men came back. Mr. Hensleigh went out to meet them. In five minutes he returned. "It's done," he said. "We begin to move to-morrow morning."

Corona gasped. She turned as pale as a water lily.

"To-morrer mornin'?" cried Puelvir. "Ye can't move this house to-morrer mornin', nohow."

"Ah," said Hensleigh indulgently, "and why not, Puelvir?"

"It's ironin' day," replied Puelvir loftily. All the reverence, all the traditions of
the New Englander concerning the third
day of the week were in her words. The
house-mover observed Puelvir with some
keen admiration.

"Your folks are lucky to have one of
your sort, miss. I don't doubt they appreciate you. I should."

Puelvir blushed, and bridled like an old
horse in a coltish moment. She could not
remember when anybody had called her
"Miss" before.

"You can go right on ironin' if you
wanter," continued the house-mover, "all
the same. Folks do. Some prefer it."

"What? Me live in my house while
we're sailin' over?" cried Puelvir gleefully.
"Land! Miss Corona, I'm a-goin' to do it.
I'll be starched if I won't!"

"George, you'll have to saw that kitchen
off," added the house-mover. "The hull
thing won't set on one scow. And you'll
have to take down yer pictures an' crockery,

Miss Corona. I s'pose you don't calc'late to stay aboard, even if that other lady does. You 'd better move out as soon as possible."

"Well, I don't know about that," replied Hensleigh. "We don't get this every day. What do you say, Corona? I gave up Cape Breton, and here 's a comic opera yachting trip providentially offered upon the altar of my unselfishness. Shall we stay aboard — with Puelvir?"

"I 'm ready," said Corona a little sentimentally. "I 'm ready to stand by Paradise."

"I would n't miss the experience for a good deal," answered Hensleigh with rising spirit. "Sir, you may prepare to move us all."

"Jes' as you say," returned the mover with a meaning glance at Mr. Timbers. "I hope ye won't have too much on't."

"Don't forget my clothes-post," called Puelvir from the kitchen door. "That 's got to go! An' say! Be we goin' to leave the hogshead 'n' the coal bin behind us?

An' what 'll I do with my wash-tubs 'n' all
that truck under the house?"

"Will I drive The Lady around?" asked
Zero feebly, "or are you goin' to freight
her 'n' the buggy over?"

"Why, Zero!" asked Corona tearfully,
"what are you crying about?"

"He thinks he's lost his sitiwation," explained Puelvir. "He thinks he can't walk
no seven miles twic't a day to 'n' fro. I
told him you'd camp him out someways. I
never knew you go back on nobody."

"Why, we'll build him a little room,"
interrupted Hensleigh carelessly.

When it became known in Fairharbor
that Paradise was to be moved — and
moved by water — public sentiment fer-
mented. Half the population of the Point
was on the ground at seven o'clock the next
morning when Mr. Timbers and the house-
mover arrived. The only conspicuous ab-
sentee was the landlord.

That day the temporary "way" or trestle
was put up, upon which Paradise was to

slide into the harbor. The day after the two scows backed up against the rocky headland and complacently observed the furore that their unprecedented appearance occasioned. Coincident with this the house-mover and a large gang put their desecrating hands upon the foundations of Paradise. The building trembled. Trellis and sheathing were ruthlessly cut away. The china tinkled. Lamps tottered. Pictures swayed, and books dropped from their cases. Matthew Launcelot made for the house-mover with a terrific howl. Hensleigh watched the proceedings with scientific serenity. But Corona turned pale. Puelvir was wildly excited. She ran from room to room, sticking her head out of every window in the house. The great jacks began to writhe and creak. Paradise thrilled and groaned. There was a slow, sickening, upward motion of the building. Puelvir, in an ecstasy, cried out: —

"Well, if he's rose, he'll find out we've rose too!"

She ran back to her kitchen. The door
was opened into it from the dining-room.
She looked and then uttered a great cry
that rang even above the orders of the
mover, the stretching of the ropes, the clank
of the windlass, and the shouts of the landlord, who was vainly trying to keep hordes
of excited sightseers away from his cabbages.
"Hold on! Stop there, mister! You 've
left my house behind!"

The kitchen had been sawed through so
deftly while she was making the beds that
its excision had escaped Puelvir's notice.
As the main house rose, the kitchen, with
an indifferent air, remained *in statu quo.*
Puelvir could hardly credit her senses.
Little by little, like a nightmare, the kitchen
door grew small and smaller. Would she
be shut out of her own house forever? Her
precious kitchen, her new kitchen, and the
bedroom on top! The maroon and indigo
curtains! A blind instinct took Puelvir,
and with a gaunt leap like a kangaroo she
plunged down through the narrowing door-

way, past the widening space, into her own domain.

"Ef you leave this here kitchen behind you leave me!"

Puelvir set her arms akimbo defiantly, but big, angry tears were rolling down her cheeks.

"There, there, Puelvir," sobbed Corona, "I *told* you the kitchen should go too. Come here and help me, quick! The vases are on their heads. The water pitchers are all wobbling. Oh, see the water leaking through the ceiling — and the teacups " —

The house swayed and lurched. The family gathered wildly to protect their altars and fires. Matthew Launcelot's maddening howls rose above the din.

Mr. Hensleigh laid all the pictures carefully upon all the beds, and then sat down hard on several and broke the glass. Corona put all her best china between the sofa pillows, and Puelvir laid two coal-hods and Johnson's big Atlas on top of them. A mental aberration seized the household like that which possesses a family when the house is on fire.

And now the cottage rolled out towards the water. The excitement became intense. Mad cheers arose from the spectators. But the mover's lips tightened apprehensively.

"We've got to resk her, Bill," he muttered to his foreman. "If the tide drops on us before we get her on to them scows it'll be an all-night job of it, and plenty of it, too."

Hensleigh watched the process with great anxiety. Supposing Paradise should be lurched into the bay at the last moment! Happily, the women of the family knew nothing of any such possibility.

The tide was high at six, and it was now nearly that hour. The two scows leaned expectantly towards their approaching burden. They were lashed together and anchored to the granite cliffs. A little out beyond the traps a fussy tug officiously blew off steam, as if protesting against a miscalculation that everybody seemed to expect.

And now the kitchen L tagged after the

house valiantly, like a seine-boat towed by a lazy schooner. Puelvir and Zero stood sculptured in the open space where the wall had been sawed off. Mr. and Mrs. Hensleigh and Matthew Launcelot occupied the main house. The crowd watched breathlessly. Hensleigh consumed his tenth cigar. But Corona, who could not smoke, trembled.

All at once Paradise gave a great dip. The scows swayed ominously. The tug backed up with its huge warp ready for a strong pull.

"Lord have mercy on us for a fambly of fools and loonys! Here we be!" cried Puelvir hysterically.

And now the kitchen L followed its leader obediently. The tide had fallen half an hour. One side of the flat scows was held up upon a jut in the rocks. When Puelvir's L was slowly adjusted to its place the scows tipped still farther over with the added weight. The captain of the tug, from the pilot-house, shook his head ominously. If the scows stuck and could not be pulled off, he knew the chances were that at the fall of the tide Paradise would be utterly wrecked. He blew three impatient blasts.

"All aboard!" shouted the mover. "Don't mind jacks nor ways nor nothing! Let her go, quick!"

The blue water foamed, and the tug churned as she had never churned before. The two scows groaned and crunched and slid, and held, and slid again, and held once more. Hensleigh and Corona looked at each other. He was so disturbed that she tried to comfort him. A moment would decide the fate of Paradise.

Then the captain of the tug shouted to the fireman, and the fireman, who had been looking out of his side door, disappeared. The screw turned as if it would strain itself into an apoplexy. The hawsers cracked. The scows scraped — scraped — and were free. There was a great splash. There was a sudden sinking — Corona thought it

was their destruction, but Hensleigh knew it
was their salvation. Puelvir shrieked, but
Zero was as mute as a monkfish.

"We'll be drownded!" cried Puelvir,
prancing about the kitchen like a maniac.
But the fireman of the tug looked at her,
and with a kind gesture of his big hand
comforted her.

"Well," said Alexander, with a sigh of
relief, "we're afloat now and as safe as can
be. Let's take one more look at the old
place and bid it good-by. We'll have a
better soon, dear."

Corona sighed, and leaning on her husband's arm she turned to look. Behind
them sloped a desolated rock. The hogshead and the coal bin ornamented the per-
spective. The landlord bowed unmoved
among the cabbages. The water widened.

"Stop! Whoa! Back! We've gotter
go back!" shrieked Puelvir suddenly.
"Mr. Hensleigh, they've gotter go back!
Whoa, there! Whoa! They've fergotten
my clothes-post!"

"Go and get supper, Puelvir," said the mistress authoritatively. "Light your kerosene stove, and do the best you can."

But still the water widened, foam flew, and the sea looked black. Corona and her husband watched the receding shore in silence. At that moment a carriage rolled up to the clothes-post. A gentleman got out — then a lady — then a child. They looked perplexedly about them.

"It 's Tom!" cried Corona. "It 's Tom and Susy — and the baby — come to make us a visit!"

CHAPTER IX

PARADISE LOST

"WELL, this is a pretty piece of business!" Tom sat resting on his oars, his handsome, good-natured face dripping profusely with the unexpected exercise, and contracted into something that was not a smile. Tom had put Susy and the baby into the first boat that he could lay hands on, and had rowed violently out into the wake of Paradise.

"I say, Alexander Hensleigh, what are you doing with my sister?" Tom's only explanation of the sight before him was that Corona had married a madman. He looked quite fierce — for Tom.

Corona and Hensleigh gazed down upon their relatives from a superior height. The dirty scow towered above the little cedar boat. Corona looked at Susy and did not say a word. Susy looked up at her sister-in-law with unutterable reproach. Nothing in the English language presented itself to Corona's mind as equal to the situation.

"You — see — we thought we'd move," she explained fatuously.

"It's cheaper by water," exclaimed Alexander with an embarrassed air.

At this inopportune moment Puelvir, who was getting supper, and who had heard nothing of this unfortunate arrival, opened the kitchen window with a bang. In this half hour she had already acquired the nautical habit of throwing things overboard. Happily, it was only a pan of strawberry hulls, but these landed directly on the baby's head and tumbled all over her little spic-and-span dress.

What was merely a trifling coolness before now threatened to become an Arctic family breach. Susy was greatly offended. The little girl's clothes were spattered all over, red and ruined. She looked as if she had come from a battlefield. Susy angrily tried to pick off the hulls with her white gloves on. Tom leaned on his oars and burst into peals of laughter. Puelvir's hoarse apologies made a background to the catastrophe.

"Here, Mr. Hensleigh," she ordered, "you go take them pictur' glasses, 'n' water pitchers, 'n' them two ker'sene lamps off the front bed, an' I 'll slick it right up for 'em. You, down there, climb up some way; I 'll give ye a good supper, and afterward I 'll wash the baby all out, bless her! an' do her up again!"

"Thank you, Puelvir," said Susy with unnecessary dignity. "We have had quite enough of your hospitality. We will go to the hotel. Pull away, Tom!"

Here Hensleigh and Corona recovered their smitten senses. They cried out in one breath: —

"Come aboard. Do come and stay all night! — move up with us — stay a week! Take supper, anyway!"

"I 've got griddle cakes," urged Puelvir persuasively.

"There 's maple sorop!" called Zero earnestly, as if this were an unanswerable argument.

The engineer of the tug put his head out of his little window and laughed. The deck hands grinned.

"Shut up there!" the house-mover said with unnatural solemnity.

This nautical appreciation of the situation did not soothe Susy. She shook her head sternly, turned it away, and sank back in her seat.

"Put about!" she continued to Tom. "The idea of expecting me to climb twenty feet up that dirty scow with this dress on, and the baby. I would n't risk the baby on that thing " —

"There, there, my dear!" said Tom patiently. He looked a little disappointed, but he was a good American husband, and accustomed to obey his wife and keep peace in the family.

"Never mind, Sis, old girl; I 'll see you in the morning," he called out cheerily.

"By the way," he shouted when he had rowed about a hundred feet, "whereabouts on the map of New England are you going to bring up?"

"Squall River!" yelled back Zero, in behalf of the family. Zero could always hear on the water.

.   .   .   .

Corona and Alexander, when their relatives had gone, settled back upon the piazza and looked at each other blankly. This episode had stupefied them both. The evening air was calm, with just enough zest of the sea and invigoration in it to make it a quick anæsthetic to any mental turmoil. They had decided to eat their supper on the piazza, and Puelvir now came out of the kitchen and across the gang plank, which united the two scows, bearing a tray in her sinewy arms, and muttering subdued imprecations on the folly of their late guests. She presented her employers with a kerosene stove supper of hot griddle cakes and cold strawberries. The piazza bobbed up

and down gently while they ate. The tide
gurgled under the two scows. The tug cut
the water with a slow, indifferent motion.
Paradise Point receded obviously. The
mouth of Squall River yawned ahead. The
sun was setting. The harbor was as calm
as a washbowl.

"You're not seasick, are you, dear?"
asked Hensleigh anxiously.

"N—no," replied Corona. She might
have said that she was homesick; but she
did not.

Alexander was in the act of swallowing
his last strawberry, and was feeling particu-
larly happy and peaceful and at home, when
there was a tremendous splash. This was
synchronously accompanied by a loud, virulent hissing of steam. Corona sprang to
her feet. Matthew Launcelot was already
on his. This voyage had been a great
strain on Matthew. His little black and
tan heart had almost beat itself out in this
excitement. He had been accustomed to
burglars who took away a portion of the

house, but these malefactors who took away the whole house bodily would have puzzled the imagination of the best watchdog in New England.

"Something terrible has happened!" cried Corona, paling.

"It's only the anchor overboard, and the tug — she's letting off steam," explained the house-mover paternally. "Here ye are, safe fur the night on the edge of the channel, and everything is all right!" The house-mover put so much relief into this last clause that Corona began to understand the strain that he had undergone in this novel experiment. She sank back into her chair with a tremulous exclamation of gratitude. But Matthew Launcelot was not to be appeased by soft explanations. He made a dive to the side of the scow to which the tug was lashed. There was no rail, and the exhaust steam, as it came hissing from below, obscured the edge of the platform. The dog gave an angry leap into the white, hot fog — with a shriek disappeared over the side of the scow — and with a little but significant splash fell into the churning water.

Every owner of a dog knows the cry that only terror and danger can evolve from a canine throat. Dogs talk with as much expression as people. Corona this time knew that some real trouble had happened. She ran to the side of the piazza towards the tug. Puelvir, who had also been well trained in the canine vocabulary, dashed down the improvised steps of her detached kitchen. The engineer of the tug shut off the steam.

"Save him! Save him! Save him!" cried Corona, wringing her hands. "He's all I have!"

At this remark, the unconscious survival of her maiden days, Alexander shut his lips together hard.

"Shall I jump in after him?" he asked perfunctorily. He began to unbutton his coat.

"N—no"—

Hensleigh threw his coat off.

"No! No! *No!*" Corona cast her arms about his neck. Alexander struck a heroic attitude, and looked much pleased.

"He's sunk!" shrieked Puelvir consolingly.

"He's gone down twic't," drawled Zero leisurely.

"Good riddance!" muttered the house-mover, trying to look troubled, but instinctively feeling of his shins.

At this agonized moment the engineer of the tug caught sight of the little struggling figure, swirling past the stern of his boat. He ran to the rail, hurled himself over, held on by one hand and one foot, and stretched himself to his full length. He had little space to spare. As it was, there was half an engineer under the water; but his big, brawny hand caught the dog by his tail, and swooped him up as if he had been a bit of waste. Dripping, handsome, nonchalant, the engineer held the terrier up by the nape of his neck, and tossed him upon

the scow at Corona's feet.   For once in his
life Matthew would not stay to be kissed
and cried over.   He slipped from his mistress' embrace, and hunted the two scows all '
over until he found the house-mover.   Then
he bit that worthy mechanic incisively in
the leg, with the immovable conviction that
it was all his fault.   Hensleigh did not
know it, but that assault added fifty dollars
to his bill.

Now Puelvir looked upon the engineer
with much compassion.   In her imagination
he was an important nautical character.
She had read of great deeds done at sea,
and now one had been enacted before her
very eyes.

"I'm sure," she said to him enthusiasti-
cally, "the critter wa'n't wuth the awful
resk."   The deck hands smiled audibly, but
Puelvir loftily ignored them.

"I wish it was you I'd saved," answered
the engineer gallantly.   "Then it would
have been something like."

"It wa'n't nothing at all," said the house-mover with unnecessary decision. "Look at me. I 've hed worse resk 'n he has. I 'd 'a' done that myself!"

"Why did n't you, then?" retorted Puelvir, looking from one mechanic to the other with the coquetry that only half a century's experience can give. Then she deliberately turned her back on the landsman, and gazed softly down at her nautical hero.

"Had n't I better make ye some catnip tea? Won't ye take cold?" she tenderly said. "Or, perhaps, ye 'd rather let yer wife fix ye up?" she added sadly.

"No such luck for me. I wish I had!" returned the engineer.

"Then mebbe you 'd eat a griddle cake," said Puelvir, blushing; "an' I 'll run upstairs an' get a dry pair of Mr. Hensleigh's fur ye."

"Not for Joseph!" protested the engineer. "But I *will* take one o' them griddle cakes."

In a few minutes, to the envy of all the deck hands and to the consternation of the house-mover, Puelvir passed down to the engineer a heaping plate of steaming griddle cakes, swimming in Corona's most expensive maple syrup.

"I never ate the like of them before," said the engineer with ecstatic solemnity when the plate was empty. "The next time I get a chance I'll take another; and the next time I'll take you!"

By this time the captain of the tug, with the aid of the builder and house-mover, had securely anchored the scows, and had attached to the front piazza a white headlight, as prescribed by law for anchored craft. The water was now alive with spectators in little boats. Such a flitting had never been seen in Fairharbor, and the house-mover was the hero of the day. Mr. and Mrs. Hensleigh felt themselves to be very inferior characters in this public drama. Nobody paid any particular attention to them — not even their own employees, who proceeded with expert independence to make all the arrangements for the night.

The captain now gave notice that he was going to steam to his regular wharf in the inner harbor, and leave them for the night.

"We always do," he explained to Corona, who objected to being left alone with no visible means of locomotion or protection. "I'd have to charge you twenty-five dollars extra, if I laid alongside here; besides, it wouldn't do nohow; it would be a bad precedent for scows."

"But we're not scows!" blazed Corona.

"It's all the same to us folks," waived the captain, sounding several blasts of the whistle to clear a way among the small boats. "Ye couldn't have a safer nor a fairer night, if ye chose out of the hull year."

"Remember, dearest, I'm here to protect you," added Hensleigh with his tenderest air.

"Y—yes," said Corona doubtfully. "But, Mr. Timbers, won't you stay with us — and the mover, too?"

The mechanics shook their heads. With

a final glance of inspection they stepped
aboard the tug. "'T ain't necessary," said
the builder.

"I 've got to milk two cows," said the
house-mover, "and I 'm late already."

Without Corona's knowing it, the tug
had cast off, and imperceptibly moved away
from Paradise. The fleet of little boats
turned to follow the tug.

"You 're all right!" shouted a cheerful
fisherman. "Norman's Woe ain't safer 'n
you be."

Another husky voice took up the theme.
This came from the red dory of an eel-
spearer. "Ye 're faster where ye be than
the whistlin' buoy. Ye 'd hang there, a
night like this, with a cod-hook. There
ain't an air, and there won't be none."

But Father Morrison, from his green
lobster-boat, wet the forefinger of his right
hand and turned it to all points of the compass. Then he shook his head sagely. He
did not speak. His last nautical experience
with the Hensleigh family had created in

Father Morrison an unprecedented humility. He rowed home without communicating with Paradise, for he did not want Mrs. Hensleigh to ask him what he thought about the weather.

Left to themselves for the first time, the family began to make strenuous preparations for the night. As Puelvir's house was entirely open to public view where it had been sawed off, her maiden meditations were a good deal disturbed. She took down her maroon and indigo curtains from her windows, and hung them at full width across the opening. As these did not suffice, she nailed up some sheets and a red and white patchwork bed quilt. Upon her windows she modestly pasted several copies of the Fairharbor "Evening Gale." Then, having satisfactorily inspected these arrangements, she sat down upon her bed and began to crimp her hair. She only did this on great occasions. Puelvir was thinking of the engineer.

"Where's Zero?" cried Corona suddenly, from the main house; "we can't find him anywhere!"

Puelvir put her head out between the bedquilt and the curtains. Lucky for the engineer that he did n't see her then! "Zero? Why, he's plumb, dumb asleep this half hour. I slung him up in a hammock in the woodshed!"

"I hope he'll take very good care of you, Puelvir, dear," said Corona. "Mr. Hensleigh says we're perfectly safe!" she quavered. She was very uneasy. Even Alexander could not comfort her. It seemed to her as if the scow might yawn at any moment and let them through. As a potent protection against such a catastrophe she went all over the house and locked it up three times. The strange harbor lights, the sickening sway of the sea, the dipping of the house that suggested implacable forces, the cries of the sailors from good, honest boats anchored near, even the familiar odor of her husband's cigar — all these made the woman sick at heart.

But Alexander was in his element. He stalked the piazza proudly. He felt as if he were captain of a man-of-war. His wife had to call him three times to come in; and when at last he locked the front door for the night it was with a sigh of genuine regret that he mounted the swaying stairs.

"Where *are* you, dear?" asked Corona tremulously.

"I'm coming up the companion-way," replied Alexander.

In spite of the strangeness of the situation the family slept soundly that night. They were completely tired out. It might have been two o'clock in the morning that Alexander was awakened by a sharp, terrified barking. Matthew Launcelot was at the window. With one bound Hensleigh jumped to his feet. To his surprise, the house was lurching violently. He stumbled over the dog, and threw up the window. A terrible gust of wind smote him in the face and almost strangled him. He could dimly see that the harbor was white-capped, and amid the shrieking of the wind he could hear the straining clank of the chains of the adjacent schooners.

Corona had now scrambled to his side. She was completely dressed. So great was her apprehension that she had thrown herself upon the bed in her clothes.

"This is terrible!" she shouted. But she might as well have whispered. Her breath was swept away in the roar of the wind.

"Come!" cried Hensleigh. He gripped his wife authoritatively by the arm, and they pitched downstairs and out on the piazza. The dog followed them, trembling and whining. The scene that met them was indeed frightful. They held to the railing, expecting to go overboard at any moment. The two scows heaved unevenly. The ropes that bound them together cracked, and at every motion the scows brought up upon the single anchor and upon themselves, with sickening jerks.

Hensleigh put his arms about his wife.

At that moment the squall gave Paradise a merciless blow. There was a snap, and then a sudden bound.

"My God!" cried Hensleigh, "she's parted!"

Twenty Pound Light rushed by like a race-horse. The two struggled to the end of the piazza. When they got there they looked for their kitchen L. Instead, was darkness, and rushing of waters. The scow, the kitchen, Puelvir and Zero had disappeared. The occupants of Paradise were alone, and headed out to sea.

CHAPTER X

PARADISE FOUND

WHEN Alexander found his lares and penates adrift, and headed, in the blackness of the storm, out to sea, his first feeling was a suffocation of conscience. To begin with, he had married this woman; to an imagination, that seemed at this moment of disaster as turbulent as the angry waves upon which they tossed, misfortune had followed them almost from the hour of his alliance. Had he not nearly burned Paradise up? Was it not his fault alone that the landlord had made a raise, unheard of in the annals of real estate? And was not this followed by the placing of Paradise Point in the march of progress? He — Hensleigh — had been the serpent in Eden, and he alone. And, to cap the climax of his responsibility, had he not engaged the mover, hired the scows, bought the lot, and launched Paradise upon this mad risk? Thus, in the first shock of this terrible squall, when he expected to be cast upon the foam-tossed rocks that are so artistic under a summer sun, and so deadly under an easterly gale, he clasped his wife convulsively to his bosom, while, at the same time, he blamed himself most bitterly that he had been the innocent means of bringing — oh, not only her precious home, but her own dear self, into this deadly peril. Thus in the blast, in the night, in the dash of the spray, and in the creaking and groaning and whistling and rocking of the scow, — in the very blossom of their honeymoon, — they kissed as if it were for the last time their lips should meet on earth.

In the course of these reflections and endearments it occurred to Alexander that they were not drowned yet. He unclasped his arms, and discovered in the process that he had been enfolding Matthew Launcelot in the same embrace with his wife. While this discovery did not thrill him, still he was pleased to know that, so far, not one of his immediate family was lost. He howled into Corona's ear: —

"If you can hold on to this piazza railing, I will see what I can do!" He proceeded to untie the lantern that was swinging a mad protest and warning from the piazza roof. Hensleigh remembered that there was a large coil of rope aboard, and also a spare anchor, which it had not seemed necessary to those experts to put out. Having been a yachtsman in his younger days, Hensleigh found this a familiar combination, and he knew what to do with it. But Corona had no idea of being left alone. She was none of your namby-pamby sort of women, who faint at peril through sheer nerve cowardice. She had often pictured herself in every variety of danger and what she would do therein. True, she had never pictured this variety. Nevertheless, the mind-training that she had given herself was not lost even in this unheard-of emergency.

"Some one must be called!" she said.

She staggered into the swaying house, made her reeling way to the china-closet shelf, and set her trembling hand upon the dinner bell. Hensleigh was at this moment tying a sailor's hitch upon the ring of the anchor. Holding Matthew Launcelot with one hand and the bell with the other, Corona closed the front door and made her way, almost on her hands and knees, toward the flickering light near which her husband was bending.

"Somebody may hear us and save us," she screamed. "I'm going to ring. Hullo! Help! Puelvir! Zero! Mr. Timbers!" Matthew Launcelot, recovering from the limpness of mortal terror, roused himself to sudden vociferation.

The dog's bark and the dinner bell rose discordantly together. It was Puelvir's big kitchen bell, the one that she used when people were out of doors and late to meals. But only the rage of the squall replied.

"She's drowned," thought Corona, with a ghastly calm. "This proves it."

Alexander was working to windward, and

it is doubtful whether he heard either wife or dog or bell. He did not look up. But Corona looked to leeward. In the lashing of foam and in the rift of the darkness she thought she saw a green light. She did not know that this was the starboard lantern of a schooner beating into harbor, close rigged, in the teeth of the squall. Corona, quite beside herself, stared at the approaching green light. She did not know what she said. She called out in a shrill, feminine quaver: —

"Oh, please don't run into us! · We're only a house adrift! We can't stop! Whoa!"

Whether the look-out saw the unsteady lantern, or whether he heard the yapping of the dog or the clang of the dinner bell, — strange sounds at dead of night to be driving with a squall, and to be borne upon the spray to his alert ears, — at any rate, he gave a hoarse signal to the two men at the wheel.

Threatening, — like a huge nightmare bat,

— frightful, imposing, hissing, the three-master bore away, and then came about with Paradise under its lee. You might have thrown Matthew Launcelot on board, so close the apparition came. Fear-stricken sailors bent over the lee rail and cast incredulous looks at the loaded scow. What must their thoughts have been to see a house loom up in the middle of the harbor on a night like this? But Corona fell by her husband's side. Both were dumb before their danger.

The hissing night swallowed the schooner, and was blacker than before.

"Help me, Corona!" cried her husband. "Quick! It's all the chance we have. We must get this anchor out, or go to the bottom!"

Corona responded bravely. Hensleigh had taken the precaution to make the other end of the rope fast to the nearest object that he thought would hold. He had made a hitch over a great joist that supported the house upon the scow. It was a half hitch, and he might have been very proud of it. But the anchor weighed a hundred pounds, and was in an awkward position. Hensleigh tugged and pulled. Corona poked and shoved. At that moment the gale gave an angry blast, more fierce, more virulent than any that had preceded it. Under its force the scow took on increased impetus. Hensleigh was now thoroughly frightened. He gave a mighty hoist. There was a splash, a gurgle, a pause, and then a tremendous wrench that seemed to shake Paradise from her very foundations. Windows cracked, blinds rattled, and china and pictures and furniture and doors reëchoed and slammed.

Where were Hensleigh and Corona? Prostrate beneath the straining rope that had saved their lives. At this moment, as if with Providence prepense, the wind stopped, and the calm came.

"Matthew!" called Corona faintly. Her hand was in her husband's, but her arms were empty of her dog.

"Matthew Launcelot! We're all right.

Matthew; come here, sir! Whee-ee-e, sir!'"

But Matthew did not respond to this half-strangled whistle. Corona groped around in the darkness on the scow. But the dog was gone.

. . . .

Puelvir woke up shivering. The first blast of the squall had battered down the scant protection of curtains and blankets that she had pinned up, and had left her room entirely open on one side to the roaring blackness of the furious night. Puelvir's modesty was shocked. She sprang up to refasten the curtains. She found herself in the middle of a whirlwind. First the towels and stockings revolved about the room, and then sped out the open side. These were followed by sheets, pillow-cases, curtains, aprons, blankets, chairs, and table, until Puelvir felt herself irresistibly sucked into the cyclone, and almost swept out of her room. All this took only a few moments from the time of her awaking. Then came the breaking of the cable, and the sundering of the two scows. Puelvir dimly understood what these accidents portended. She had rushed to the door that led downstairs to the kitchen. It was held by the wind, and she could hardly open it from the inside. In the struggle she began to call out hoarsely: —

"Get up there, Zero! We're shipwrecked! The kitchen's overboard!"

But Zero did not answer. He was slumbering peacefully in his hammock, which did not sway with the scow. For Zero had once been on a trip to the Grand Banks as cook's boy, and neither the motion nor the commotion was sufficient to disturb his dreams. At last, Puelvir, breathing heavily, arrived at the woodshed, and began to shake the hammock violently.

"Git up!" she called. "The kitchen's gone bust into the Atlantic Ocean, and it's blowin' like all possessed outside! Don't ye hear it?"

"Hay?" asked Zero mildly. "It's too early to get up yet. Lemme alone."

But Puelvir, without ceremony, lifted up one side of the hammock, and spilled Zero flatly out on the heaving floor. The gale roared. The kitchen trembled and shook. Puelvir thought that they were about to be bodily blown into the sea. So she stood up as firmly as she could, and grasped the side of the shed, to hold it down. But Zero, whose intelligence, like that of all Fairharbor boys, burned (like potassium) brightest upon water, cocked up his head and listened, and then scrambled to his feet.

"It's a squall," he said coolly. "I'll go on deck and look out for her."

When Puelvir struggled on deck and found Paradise gone, she was overwhelmed by a stupor of fear, not so much for herself as for the safety of her mistress:

"She's drownded!" wailed Puelvir, beating her hands upon her breast. "She can't do nothin' without me. She never could. *He's* no good!" To her mind the husband had always been a useless encumbrance. Now Puelvir looked upon him as little less

than a murderer. That her dear Miss Corona should be separated from her under
these dreadful circumstances, and with him,
was more than she could bear. As for herself, it had not yet occurred to her to be
very much frightened on her own account.
She did not know enough to know what
danger she was in. But Zero understood
that they were in desperate straits.

"We've got to hold her, or she'll bring
up on Halfway Rock, and go to kindling!"
he roared at Puelvir, with an idea of giving
her comfort.

As they were in total darkness, the main
house having gone off with their only lantern, Zero labored at a considerable dis-
advantage. Besides, there was no anchor
aboard, and no warp to anchor with if there
had been one. Zero was greatly perplexed.
But, as he had never been in sole command
of a craft before, and as he had seen worse
gales at sea and more water aboard, he un-
dertook his new responsibility with great
zest and some sense.

"This ain't nothin'!" he bellowed again into Puelvir's face. "I've seen worse than this. If I only hed an anchor, an' a road, an' rock bottom, we'd fetch her up soon enough." He crawled around to the great wooden cleats upon which the warp had been fastened that held the anchor before it parted. Zero felt of the rope, and began to pull it in. To his surprise, it pulled hard, and before he knew it he had about fifteen fathoms of good cable aboard. It had evidently got fouled on the fluke of the anchor, and been chafed off there by the strain. Puelvir knew nothing of this find. She stood with her gaunt hands making telescopes at her eyes, peering into the storm. "If she had n't gone and got married"—she muttered bitterly to herself.

"I want an anchor!" Zero came up and bellowed this request into Puelvir's face, as if he had been asking for a dish-towel or a quart measure.

"Why don't ye take the stove?" sobbed Puelvir. "It's heavy enough. I won't

need it no more.   We sha'n't never see her
again."

"It mought do," said Zero doubtfully.
"We mought catch on sumthin'.   I hain't
heard of none bein' used that way.   There
ain't no harm tryin'.   Gimme a lift!"

The scow danced and spun in the gale.
It was now far out in the harbor.   Puelvir began to be thoroughly alarmed.   She
could see nothing in the blackness.   She
could feel the salt tears wetting her cheeks
like rain.   She helped eagerly at the stove.
Zero pulled at the legs, which were of the
kind that stay on.   The open side of the
sawed-off kitchen made it easy to get the
stove out and down upon the scow.   The
muscles stood out on Puelvir's big, strong
arms.   She lifted and tugged like a man.

"I 'll tie the line on," she said, panting.
"It 's my stove."

"No, ye don't," Zero retorted.   "It 's
my ship!   Get out!   You 'll tie a granny."

"Call me a granny?"   Puelvir wrath-
fully lifted up her hand to box the boy's

ears. But at that moment a wail came over the sea. It was the tolling of a bell. She thought she recognized the sound.

"It's the dinner bell!" she cried out. "Miss Corona's callin' of me! Hi there! Miss Corona! Here I be!"

"Rats!" interrupted Zero. " Here, gimme a hand on this here stove. It's the bell-buoy off Norman's Woe. If ye don't heave her over now we're goners sure!"

This practical hint as to their saline status sobered Puelvir like a dash of sea water. Choking, sobbing, dazed by gale and sea, and loss and terror, she gave the stove a mighty heave. It went over with a splash that sounded above the squall. The wind struck them more incisively than before. The bell now tolled wild and menacing. It came nearer and nearer. Zero, in the meanwhile, was feeling of the cable as the scow dragged the stove on the uneven bottom. Suddenly there was a terrible bump — a howl of the bell enveloped them — a final shriek of the squall — a surging

and wrenching of the scow, and a slipping
of the kitchen followed. The two were
thrown from their feet. Zero was the first
to recover himself.

"We're all right!" he yelled above the
storm. "We've brought up on the buoy.
We've give her a good crack. We've
knocked the stuffin' out of her! The stove
has fouled her chain! Our anchor is
ketched! Bully for us!"

.   .   .   .

July never blossomed into a lovelier,
calmer dawn than it did on the morning
following this historic squall. The wrecks
of gilded yachts, of trim fishermen, and of
lumbering coasters strewed the harbors from
Boston to Portsmouth. Fairharbor was sig-
nally free from loss of craft and life. Only
two yachts had dragged ashore.

At the earliest gray of the morning, long
before the lobster men go to inspect their
pots, long before the traps are hauled, or
sloops leave their weirs for the early market,
two tugs, whose black smoke seemed even

in the flying darkness to desecrate the purity
of the bay, coincidentally put their wheels
hard down, signaled "full speed," and made
for the objects of their long search. One
tug was scouring the harbor; the other was
coming in after a fruitless trip at sea.
Since two o'clock these anxious guardians
of the harbor had been vainly searching for
Paradise, which, in its detached form, they
must have passed and repassed in the harbor
many times. In a little cove by the beach,
sheltered and serene, within a biscuit's
throw of a summer cottage, Paradise floated
peacefully. Towards it Mr. Timbers and
the house-mover, on the harbor tug, made
a straight course. Quaking with the terrors
of a broken contract, and the expected re-
proaches of an offended woman, they urged
the tug to its best speed.

On the other side of the harbor — two
miles out — on the edge of the channel, the
bell-buoy lazily called. Here a touching
meeting was taking place.

The captain of the tug that had been

engaged to move the cottage leaned far out of his pilot-house, giving orders to make her fast, and to hold her this time with all the warps on board. The engineer, having shut off steam, was the first to board the derelict. He and Puelvir met on the scow's deck and wrung each other's hands like friends who had been separated for a long time. Zero came proudly up for the nautical recognition that he felt was due to him at this crisis.

"It *was* a blow," began the engineer, looking around and then letting his gaze rest upon Puelvir's honest face, "an' ye 've stood it, miss, like a man."

But Puelvir looked at the engineer severely, and took her hand out of his. "Where be they?" she demanded. "Is *she* safe?"

For answer the engineer turned her shoulders gently to the eastward, where Paradise floated in the cove.

"See? I guess everybody 's all right. I 'll bet there ain't another house on the coast," he said, with a bow, "that hed rid out that squall as easy as yourn. I'd rather have her than a yacht, a durn sight. But how did ye anchor her? Ye didn't have none aboard."

"Thank the Lord o' Mercy on us!" Puelvir wiped her eyes with the back of her rough hand. She was not thinking about anchors.

"We heaved over the kitchen stove," put in Zero proudly. "That ketched her!"

"Kitchen stove!" repeated the engineer. "Well, I'll be slivered! Well, Zero, you are a sailor, an' no mistake! You're a scale of the old fish!"

"It was my idee," said Puelvir, recovering herself — "but law! let the boy have the credit on't."

"I allers said you was a corker!" said the engineer admiringly, as if he had known Puelvir a great many years.

"Come, boys!" called the captain, "cut the rope, and we'll get her out of this, and have her back there before folks get on to it."

"What, leave my kitchen stove to the
bottom? No, sir-ee!" Puelvir folded her
arms stoutly. "You men jest haul up that
there No. 7 Magee and set her up for me.
I 've got to get breakfast the first thing!"

A gallant shout went up from the tug,
and the stove, covered with seaweed and
patched with starfish, soon sprawled up out
of the water, and was finally hoisted on
deck, and lay with its feet in the air.

"I guess I kin fix her for ye," said the
engineer. "I reckon I kin set her up for
ye when we git started."

Puelvir gave him a grateful look.

By this time the two tugs, with their important tows, began to approach each other
in the middle of the harbor.

"Oh, Miss Corona, dear!" shouted Puelvir, brandishing her dish-towel.

But the mover took Hensleigh aside, and,
with a dark significance, pointed out to him
his famous half hitch of the night before.

"It 's lucky," he said dryly, "that the
wind blew itself out when you made her

fast. If it had blown five minutes longer that 'ere anchor would have pulled yer house and you along of her, clean into the water. Why, man, ye made her fast to the starboard skid instead o' the scow!"

"Well, it held, anyway," said Alexander, flushing. "But you need n't tell *her*, or anybody else. Have a cigar?"

The mover accepted the bribe, and smiled. He never told Corona.

The two scows approached slowly. The passengers stationed themselves on their respective decks with their handkerchiefs, as if they had just returned from a tour abroad. Instinctively the two women crept apart. Puelvir rushed to her kitchen door; Corona went into the dining-room. The scows were coming up sidewise. Puelvir bent far over and held her hand out. Corona did the same. The chasm grew less and less. Suddenly the soft hand felt itself clutched as if in a hard knot. There was a leap across the little space, and before anybody could say, "Don't!" Puelvir had boarded Paradise, and the two women were clasped in each other's arms, and were crying on each other's shoulders. Such a pleasant scene can only happen when mistress and maid are friends.

".Be you all safe?" hysterically asked Puelvir.

"All but one," replied Corona, the tears streaming down her face. "Matthew is gone. The dear little boy is drowned."

At that very moment the front door opened in a ghostly manner, and Matthew Launcelot, sniffing the morning air, sauntered out upon the piazza. Catching sight of the house-mover, he made a dive for that gentleman, to whom he evidently attributed the entire catastrophe of that tragic night. A cry of joy answered Matthew's bark, and Corona caught him ecstatically in her arms.

"He opened the door!" she cried proudly. "I shut it in the storm last night, and he must have opened it and gone in all by himself. That dog can open *anything!*"

"Ahoy there! Ship ahoy!" A gruff,

guttural cry from under the scow, behind the kitchen L, diverted at this moment the engineer from Puelvir, Puelvir from her mistress, the mistress from the dog, and the struggling dog from the house-mover. It incidentally diverted Hensleigh from the knot which the deck hand of the tug was tying to a new anchor.

"It's Father Morrison with them lobsters I ordered for breakfast," said Puelvir with dignity. "He never went back on us. Land! He's got a passenger."

She had hardly spoken when a gentleman's face appeared above the edge of the scow.

"I say, Hensleigh," rang out a merry voice, "give us a hand up! This scow is beastly slippery!"

"Why, it's Tom!" Corona dropped the dog and ran. "How on earth did you come here? I'm so glad you never knew anything about it at all until now!"

"Are you?" asked Tom serenely. "Well, I hope you'll invite me to breakfast. I am a little hungry. You see, Sis, I got up at two o'clock and started the tugs out after you. Then this ancient mariner and I have been scouring the Atlantic Ocean, and have searched all the lobster pots in the harbor for you in this confounded dory ever since. Whew! See? That's Susy over there crying her eyes out on the hotel piazza because we're none of us drowned."

CHAPTER XI

IT was the first Sunday in September. Dinner was over. Puelvir was washing the dishes. Her deep alto Sunday-school choruses rolled in refluent waves through the new pantry, the enlarged dining-room, and the comfortable piazza. Puelvir had sung a great deal during the last six weeks, and Zero had been blessed with a double allowance of desserts. Matthew Launcelot had finished his Sunday bone, and was trying to decide which of the parlor rugs he would use for a napkin. Corona lay in a hammock. This was gently swung by her husband, who lazily sat beside her. Every now and then Corona would pat the hand that held the netting, and every now and then Hensleigh would call her attention to a peculiarly perfect ring of smoke that he blew from his mouth. This attention seemed to the man quite an endearment. He felt that he was very attractive.

"I can't get over it," mused Corona, straightening herself up and looking about. "It's the same house, the same husband, but everything else is another world. I feel like Rip Van Winkle. I go to sleep in one place with one set of views, and wake up in another place with an entirely new lot. I don't get used to it yet."

"But, dear, marriage *is* another world. It is a change of venue. You look out of the same windows, but you see new scenes. It's the same old house with different views. If you can get used to that you can get used to this."

Corona sighed happily. She missed the broad, bright harbor, the voices of fishermen gossiping at their traps, the running in of neighbors, the bellow of the whistling buoy, the great palette of the sunsets on the bay, the scarlet flash of the revolving light, and the rhythm of the water that used to wash beneath her window and lull her to sleep. She thought of her maiden life, of her long, quiet, lonely evenings, of her days busy with unshared pleasures and un-comraded duties. The moving of Paradise completed the feeling that she was absolutely cut off from her past.

But she turned to her new horizon. There was Squall River, although, it must be admitted, a large mud flat at the ebb of the tide, yet consequently picturesque with clam-diggers; at its flood, it seemed like a peaceful lake. Storms could not ruffle its calm surface any more than petty misunderstandings can disturb the hearts of those who love each other. Below our two householders, to the right, rose their own pine grove, ornamented with little settees and mosquitoes. Near by, the stern of the Sandpiper patted the water softly at her new moorings. Then there was a glimpse of their lost harbor, and of the white city, of Ipswich Bay, and of the great sand dunes. Behind them lay the forest — cool, delight-

ful, and unexplored. Gray squirrels chat-
tered in it. Birds, so scanty on the wave-
washed cliffs, rioted here from bough to
bough, and flashed in colors of the zircon,
the hyacinth, the tourmaline, and the sap-
phire. These new neighbors cheerily and
warily made acquaintance, and took the
places of the old.

"Come," said Corona. She slipped from
the hammock, and, hand in hand, husband
and wife strolled together for the hundredth
time joyously over their new, old house.
They stood at the parlor window. "We
used to see the beach from here before;
don't you remember, dear? But I like the
pines." Upstairs in the blue room, between
the muslin curtains, Corona lingered for a
moment without speaking. Where the gray
drift of the downs used to undulate, soft
and alluring, with the uneasy sea line beyond, now the tops of trees, the descent of
the valley, the winding of the river, and the
smarting white of the sand dunes looked in
strangely. A little ache of homesickness

closed about Corona's heart. But she felt
an arm steal around her, and then she
looked up into her husband's face.

"You don't mind it, dear, do you?"
Alexander asked gently.

"I don't mind anything as long as I have
you!"

Their thoughts, which seemed to be one,
deviated distinctly at that moment. The
man had begun to feel a little impatient of
this happy idleness. The honeymoon was
to him only a beautiful interruption to a
busy career. He could not look upon it as
an interlude in the music of his life. It
was more like a theme on too high a plane
to be always maintained. The Wedding
March must soon give place to a symphony
in which many movements are played in
different time and key.

But to Corona these rapturous weeks had
become the necessary expression of existence. She remembered with remorse how
she had once laughed at a little bride who
cried all day the first time that her husband

left her to go to his business in town. Corona could not even imagine how it would be to live if Alexander were not always with her. Corona was not a new woman. She had no career. She had a genius for home. She was a home - making, home-loving soul. Her house had been more to her than other people's houses, and now her happiness — she turned and looked at her husband. She was convinced that he was more to her than any other husband to any other woman in the world. There was something in this rhapsody, after all. Women like Corona make the honeymoons that last.

"Shall I hitch The Lady up, or turn her aout?"

Zero's drawling voice broke the spell that the one reflective day in the week so easily casts upon loving hearts. The two looked at each other doubtfully; but as is frequently the case, the smallest member of the family decided the question. Matthew Launcelot, who, as has been said, hated the horse with all the enmity of which a black and tan heart is capable, at the mention of her name began to bark jealously. This disturbance effectually broke in upon the family peace, and like an interrupted chord it could not easily be found again.

"We might as well take a ride," said Alexander. "You may hitch her up, Zero. Put her in the beach wagon, and we'll take you over to see your mother."

.   .   .   .

Puelvir was left alone. She sat down on the new, little piazza that Mr. Hensleigh had built for her, and which, by the way, had almost won her heart over to him, and proudly surveyed "her house," incidentally condescending to notice the scenery. Puelvir wore a white cambric dress decorated with green four-leaved clovers, and a fresh white apron. Her brown neck was made the browner by one of the white cotton lace ornaments favored by her kind on Sundays, but a little band of green velvet around her throat relieved this effect. Her hair was crimped. Her eyes were happy, her mouth was kind, and Puelvir looked uncommonly well.

A crisp noise on the pine needles in the path through the grove suddenly attracted Puelvir's attention. She looked up. A man was coming toward the house. "It's a tramp!" thought Puelvir. She called on Matthew Launcelot, her natural protector, but Matthew had basely deserted her for a gray squirrel, and was half a mile away in the woods. Puelvir whisked into the kitchen and bolted the door. But when she gave, through the window, a second look at the intruder, she perceived that the tramp wore a high silk hat, pearl trousers, and a long-tailed black coat. Tan gloves covered his hands, and in one of them he swung a handsome malacca cane. When he saw her in the window, which she was locking as rapidly as possible, he smiled and lifted his hat two feet from his head. Puelvir's heart leaped above her cotton lace, and thumped against the green velvet ribbon at her throat. The engineer of the tug stood before her in his Sunday clothes.

"Why, land!" she said, flinging up the window. "You don't say! I thought you was a tramp. I was just settin' the critter on to you."

"How do you like it here in this God-forsaken place?" he asked, carefully depositing his tall hat on the window-sill and vigorously wiping his face.

"Well," replied Puelvir, "I miss my hogshead and my clothes-post. But we've got a pump 'n' hot water."

"Won't you let a feller in?" pleaded the caller.

"I mought and I moughtent," said the woman judicially. The engineer tried the door, and, finding it bolted, made as if he were about to climb in by the window. At this Puelvir flushed red.

"You keep your distance and set out there where you belong!" Puelvir's voice sounded sharp, but her eyes danced. "My folks are all out. I'm alone, an' you can't come in nohow. It's agin the rules. What 'che come for, anyway?"

"Well," answered the engineer slowly, "I felt kinder hungry, an' I wanted some more of them griddle cakes."

"Griddle cakes! I don't fry griddle cakes Sundays for nobody." Puelvir smiled expansively. "But I'll see if I can't hunt ye up some cold vittles. You'd better set down." Puelvir gave her dress a little flounce and disappeared into the pantry.

The engineer looked after her, and bit the ends of his heavy black mustache dubiously. "She's a hummer, she is," he muttered to himself, "an' no mistake."

But presently she came back, carrying with great care a cut-glass dish, in which a white, frosted work of art floated in a delicious sea of yellow custard. This tempting trifle was intended for the family's supper; but not having been acquainted with their privileges, they would not miss their loss. The engineer disposed of the floating island with admiration too deep for words. Per-

haps Corona's silver spoon and her best
Dresden saucer had something to do with
the feeling of luxurious comfort that began
to inundate the engineer's heart.

"By the great horn spoon, but you can
jest everlastingly beat the Dutch a-cook-
in'!" The visitor drew his chair up as
close to the window as possible, and bent
in. "Ye know," he said, looking at her
boldly with admiring eyes, "I said aboard
the tug I was a-comin' for some more o'
them griddle cakes, an' then I was a-comin'
for you. I reckon ye didn't think I meant
it. But I did. That soft stuff is a sight
better 'n cakes; and here I be."

"Oh, you be, be you?" said Puelvir
jauntily. "That takes two. What are
you goin' to do about it?" Puelvir took
the empty dishes, and appeared to carry
them to the sink with great calmness. But
in reality she felt as if the old world were
spinning around her middle - aged head.
Her nautical hero watched her with set lips.

"Unbolt that door!" he demanded.

"I won't," said Puelvir, turning on the hot water.

"You keep me out here like a tramp."

"You behave like one."

"You needn't think I'm hoofin' it way up here this hot day for nothin', miss," the engineer exploded. "Open that door, or I'll bust the whole shebang in!"

"Ye don't catch me!" retorted Puelvir with a toss of her head.

"I don't, hey?" Before Puelvir could realize what had happened, her visitor had vaulted in through the open window, and had taken her in his mighty arms. He gave her a resounding kiss. "I thought ye said it took two. There are times when it don't take more 'n one, an' that's a man with his mind made up."

Puelvir struggled and screamed. "Murder! Help! Fire! Tramps! Let me go!"

"Certainly," said the engineer, "if you want to." He opened his arms, and Puelvir sank upon a chair breathless.

"What," she gasped, "what would my

folks say if they cotched us in here with the door locked? Unbolt that 'ere door, quick!"

"They'd say," said the engineer, leisurely unfastening the door and opening it, "that I was a mighty lucky feller to get ye, an' they'd give us a blessin'. I was calculatin' we'd get spliced this fall, if you've no objections."

"I have," panted Puelvir.

"Name 'em!" The engineer stood over her. "I'll 'bide by 'em all."

"If that's so, there ain't no use my namin' of 'em." Puelvir's head drooped.

"I notice," said the engineer soberly, touching the sleeve of her dress with real delicacy, and dropping on one knee so that his face could be near to hers, "that you've got four-leaf clovers on your gown. Call it good luck, gal dear, won't you? Call it luck for two."

Puelvir glanced timidly at her lover's face. She saw his eyes tender with a depth of feeling that was rare to men of his hard life. She bent slightly toward him, and

this time, when he took her in his arms,
she did not object.

.   .   .   .

Mr. and Mrs. Hensleigh drove home in
the early dusk. Zero climbed out, and
went to The Lady's head. Matthew ran
from the woods. Puelvir came from the
house, and in the presence of the assem-
bled family she uttered these words: —

"Well, Miss Corona, he's come, an'
I've up 'n' gone 'n' done it. I've give
my word. I'm goin' to be married come
October."

"Dear me, Puelvir!" expostulated Corona.

"Well, I am. But I told him he needn't
expect to hev me till you go for the winter.
I wouldn't leave you nohow, not fur no
man. Besides, I told him he'd got to give
up tuggin' summers an' go to the Grand
Banks fishin'. I wouldn't look at him
'thout I stuck by you summers, says I. He
said he don't favor fishin', but he'd com-
permise on a Bar Harbor steamer. So that

fetched me, for I took it kinder thought-
ful of him. I won't give up nary one nor
t'other, so there, now! I 've fixed ye both."

.   .   .   .

Alexander and Corona stood alone together in the sea-scented, resinous dusk.

"What shall we do without her?" asked
Corona. "But I suppose we 'll board win-
ters, and can get along."

"I don't intend to board any longer than
we can help," Alexander replied quietly.
"I want my own home. Don't you?"

They looked out over the black pine
woods toward the harbor. Hensleigh walked
to the end of the piazza to close a blind.

"Come!" he called. "Come and see!"

Corona hurried to him. Her eyes followed the gesture of his hand. Between
the branches of a tall pine a red eye faded
and burned — faded and burned.

"It 's my lighthouse!" cried Corona rapturously. "It 's the flashlight on the Point.
I have missed it so! Oh, you dear old red
light! Now I feel perfectly contented."

To Corona the crimson light had always seemed like the heart of the sea.   Now it seemed like the heart of a home.

She lifted her face to her husband.

"Fun is good, Truth is better, and Love is best of all," quoted Alexander softly. Silently they clasped and kissed.

"I used to think Paradise was the house," she whispered.   "Now I find it is you."

"No, no! it is you!" he protested.

"It took us both to find it, dear."

"And it will take us both to keep it," he answered her, "for God meant it to be so."

www.ingramcontent.com/pod-product-compliance
Lightning Source LLC
Chambersburg PA
CBHW020114030726
47498CB00006B/2096